Divine Courage

Divine Cozy Mystery Series
Book 6

Hope Callaghan

hopecallaghan.com
Copyright © 2020
All rights reserved.

*****

Visit my website for new releases and special offers: hopecallaghan.com

D1706514

Acknowledgments

Thank you to these wonderful ladies who help make my books shine - Peggy H., Cindi G., Jean P., Wanda D., Barbara W., Renate P. and Alix C. for taking the time to preview *Divine Courage,* for the extra sets of eyes and for catching all of my mistakes.

A special THANKS to my reader review team:

Alice, Alta, Amary, Amy, Becky, Brenda, Carolyn, Charlene, Christine, Debbie, Denota, Devan, Diann, Grace, Helen, Jo-Ann, Jean M, Judith, Meg, Megan, Linda, Polina, Rebecca, Rita, Theresa, Valerie and Virginia.

CONTENTS

Cast of Characters

Joanna "Jo" Pepperdine. After suffering a series of heartbreaking events, Jo Pepperdine decides to open a halfway house for recently released female convicts, just outside the small town of Divine, Kansas. She assembles a small team of new friends and employees to make her dream a reality. Along the way, she comes to realize not only has she given some women a new chance at life, but she's also given herself a new lease on life.

Delta Childress. Delta is Jo's second in command. She and Jo became fast friends after Jo hired her to run the bakeshop and household. Delta is a no-nonsense asset, with a soft spot for the women who are broken, homeless, hopeless and in need of a hand up when they walk through Second Chance's doors. Although Delta isn't keen on becoming involved in the never-ending string of mysteries around town, she finds herself in over her head more often than not.

Raylene Baxter. Raylene is among the first women to come to the farm, after being released from Central State Women's Penitentiary. Raylene, a former bond agent/bounty hunter, has a knack for sleuthing out clues and helping Jo catch the bad guys.

Nash Greyson. Nash, Jo's right-hand man, is the calming force in her world of crisis. He's not necessarily on board with Jo and Delta sticking their noses into matters that are better left to the law but often finds himself right in the thick of things, rescuing Delta and Jo when circumstances careen out of control.

Gary Stein. While Delta runs the bakeshop and household, and Nash is the all-around-handyman, Gary, a retired farmer, works his magic in Jo's vegetable gardens. A widower, he finds purpose in helping Jo and the farm. Gary catches Delta's eye, and Jo wonders if there isn't a second chance...at love for Gary and Delta, too.

"You did not choose me, but I chose you and appointed you that you should go and bear fruit and that your fruit should abide, so that whatever you ask the Father in my name, he may give it to you." John 15:16 (ESV)

Prologue

"Not here. Not now." The shadowy figure lurked in the dark corner outside the deli, staring up at the lights above the hardware store.

A figure flitted past the window, moving too quickly to identify. Was it Malton? Or was it the convicted criminal? Fists clenched at the thought of a known felon living in town, in *their* town, steps away from innocent, upstanding citizens filled the watcher with rage.

The thoughts railed around and around, growing louder and more insistent. Something needed to be done. Had to be done.

Go somewhere else! Go where someone wants you.

The shadowy figure appeared again, this time moving slowly. The woman was clearly visible now, her brown hair tumbling over her shoulders as she stood in front of the window, peering down onto the street.

It was her. It was the convict...appearing as if she didn't have a care in the world. But not for long.

A plan began to form, small at first until it grew. A grim smile lifted the corners of the watcher's mouth. One way or another, the esteemed town of Divine would be rid of the criminal element, once and for all.

Chapter 1

"This is the last of it." Nash Greyson slammed the tailgate shut. "You about ready to head over?"

Jo nodded. "I think that's everything. If not, I can always run back to town later."

Nash placed a light hand on Jo's shoulder. "You didn't happen to intentionally leave something behind so you *could* use it as an excuse to check on Sherry later, did you?"

"Maybe." Jo chuckled as she wrinkled her nose. "Is it that obvious?"

"To me, it is."

Sherry Marshall, a resident at Jo's farm for former female convicts, had finally spread her wings and was venturing out on her own. A move that both thrilled and terrified Jo.

Emily, the first resident to leave, had gone to live with an aunt and uncle in Abilene. During Jo's last follow-up, she'd learned that Emily was not only surviving but thriving under the watchful eye of her family.

Sherry's path forward was the exact opposite. She didn't have the support of her family, who had cut all ties at the time of her incarceration, leaving the woman adrift.

But Sherry wasn't alone. She had the love and support of Joanna Pepperdine, Delta Childress, Jo's right-hand gal, Nash, Jo's handyman, who was so much more, and Gary, Jo's gardener, not to mention the other residents of the farm who were cheering her on and encouraging her. Because if Sherry had the courage to go out on her own and succeed, that meant they could too.

Marlee Davison, Jo's friend, had also been instrumental in helping Sherry get on her feet by hiring her as a server at her deli.

Jo was convinced God had answered her prayers when Wayne Malton, the owner of Tool Time Hardware, approached her about a vacancy at his recently renovated apartments above the hardware store.

She secretly suspected Wayne knew exactly how much Sherry could afford and had set the monthly rental rate within her reach. After crunching numbers, Jo and Sherry were thrilled to discover that not only could she afford the rent and utilities, she would also be able to save a little.

For the umpteenth time, Jo pushed aside the feeling of uneasiness. The place was perfect for Sherry and a short drive from the farm, only minutes away. Sherry wouldn't even need a car. She could walk to work. Everything was right there in downtown Divine.

"Hop in." Nash gave Jo a playful pat on the back and sneaked in a kiss.

Jo rounded the side of the truck and reached for the handle. She started to slide inside when she noticed a brightly wrapped package on the bench seat. "What's that?"

"A housewarming gift for Sherry."

"Which reminds me, I have a gift for Sherry too. I'll be right back." Jo darted to the kitchen door, nearly colliding with Delta, who was on her way out. "You were in such a tizzy to get going, you forgot about this stuff."

"Thanks, Delta. This whole move has me discombobulated. My head would fall off if it wasn't attached."

"Sherry's gonna be just fine." Delta handed Jo the gift bag and another bag. "I added a few containers of Sherry's favorite dishes. She should have enough meals to last a couple days."

"Thanks, Delta. I'm sure she'll appreciate it." Jo gave her friend a quick hug and returned to the truck. She placed the bags on the floor and motioned to the package next to her on the bench seat. "So, what did you get Sherry?"

"It's a surprise," Nash said.

"What kind of surprise?"

"You'll find out soon enough. What did you get her?"

"A surprise," Jo teased.

Nash chuckled. "I deserved that."

During the drive, the couple chatted about the businesses, and then the conversation drifted to Jo's open spots at the farm. "Pastor Murphy has a woman he's anxious for me to take in. I haven't made a decision yet. I'm still on the fence."

"Still on the fence?" Nash shot her a quick glance.

"There's something about her." Jo absentmindedly tugged on her seatbelt. "She's..." Her voice trailed off as she struggled to describe the woman.

"Not ready for the farm?" Nash suggested.

"Oh, she's ready. More than ready, according to her," Jo sighed. "The problem is that I'm not sure *we're* ready for her."

"You don't think she'll be a good fit?"

"She's a little brash, a little bossy."

"Then say no. You have your hands full without adding a difficult resident to the mix."

"True," Jo murmured as she stared out the window. "The only thing stopping me is that she has nowhere to go. She's older, and I think Pastor Murphy is having a hard time placing her. She has no money. No prospects."

To date, all of Jo's residents had been younger, in their twenties and thirties, except for Raylene Baxter, who was in her early forties.

"Older than Raylene?"

"Laverne is in her fifties."

"What's she in for?"

Jo had a strict policy of not allowing convicted murderers to live at the farm, although she'd bent the rules with Raylene, whose case was unique. Because of the circumstances behind her incarceration, she'd taken a vote from the women. They voted to allow Raylene, a former bounty hunter, to stay. Jo had never regretted her decision.

But there had been a couple others she *had* regretted, which was one of the reasons she hesitated to accept Laverne and was leaning toward going with her gut, which told her to pass.

"Forgery and stealing from her employer. She diverted funds into her own bank account. Not only is she brash and bossy, but she's also somewhat conniving. Like I said, I'm struggling with the fact she has nowhere to go."

"I'm sure you'll make the right decision. First and foremost, you need to think about what's best for the farm, for you and for the residents."

"Right."

They reached downtown. Nash circled the block and pulled into the small parking lot behind the hardware store. The first order of business was to unload the sofa and armchair donated to Jo's secondhand shop, Second Chance Mercantile.

Both pieces were in pristine condition and had been brought in by a local who was getting rid of everything and moving out of state to be closer to her grandchildren.

Jo had also managed to track down a set of barstools, which fit perfectly in Sherry's bar area.

With several purchases from the mercantile, Sherry had almost everything she needed to furnish her new home.

Wrangling the sofa up the stairs was a battle. Nash and Jo twisted and turned it several times before they were able to half-carry, half-drag it to the top of the stairs and into the apartment.

Sherry, who knew they were on the way, was waiting for them in the hall.

They set the sofa in the living room and returned to the truck to unload the armchair, as well as grab the bags of food and housewarming gifts.

Once everything was inside, Sherry rearranged the furniture several times before deeming it the perfect arrangement. "This is even better than I thought." She ran a light hand over the back of the sofa. "This sofa looks brand new."

"It's in excellent condition," Jo agreed.

"I still can't believe how lucky I am to have gotten this place. I keep pinching myself."

"How did you do for your first night alone?" Jo asked. "Did you feel safe? Were you able to sleep?"

"Like a baby. There's already someone living next door. Wayne told me he plans to finish renovating the third unit across the hall, and it will be ready by fall."

"Good. I'm glad to hear you aren't living here all alone."

"What are those?" Sherry pointed to the bags Jo had brought up.

"Food. Delta sent enough food to last for days," Jo said. "I saw some homemade chicken noodle soup, spaghetti pie, goulash. I think there's even a container of Delta's cookies and cream raspberry dream bars."

"Tell her I said thank you."

"I will." Jo placed the bags of food on the kitchen counter and then handed Sherry the gift bag. "This is for you. It's a housewarming gift."

"You shouldn't have, Jo. You've already done so much."

"I wanted to." Jo motioned to her. "Go ahead. I hope you like it."

Sherry pushed the tissue paper aside and pulled out a set of towels.

"It's a set of embroidered bath towels Delta has been working on for you."

"They're awesome," Sherry's eyes shined as she held up the pale pink towel with "SM" embroidered in white lettering. "I can't wait to hang them."

"I bought you a housewarming gift too." Nash handed Sherry the wrapped package.

"Seriously? You guys are too much." Sherry slipped her finger under the edge of the paper, carefully peeling back the tape. "I want to save the wrapping paper and keep it as a reminder of how much you've done for me, that I'm not alone."

Jo could feel her throat clog as she blinked back sudden tears. This was why she had put her heart and soul into the farm, the businesses, and the women who were in desperate need of a hand up, not a handout. This was Jo's reward, and her heart swelled with pride.

Sherry set the paper aside. "It's a brown box," she joked.

"A brown box with a special gift inside." Nash cast Jo a quick look. "I didn't run this by Jo first. I hope she approves."

Sherry lifted the lid. "There's another box." She reached inside and removed a second box, this one labeled.

Jo's eyes grew wide as she stared at it in disbelief. She said the first thing that popped into her head. "You can't give Sherry that."

Chapter 2

"It's not what you think," Nash argued. "I know Sherry isn't allowed to possess a firearm. This isn't a firearm. It's a personal protection device. Instead of bullets, it fires hard plastic projectiles."

"There are also pepper spray rounds which can be used interchangeably and would be effective in deterring one or more people." He removed the contents of the box and began explaining how it worked. "Think of it as a cross between a paintball and pellet gun. It can potentially ward off an attacker or a robber, giving Sherry time to escape or call for help."

"I don't know. I don't know why she would need something like that." Jo warily eyed the device, which looked exactly like a handgun. "Is it even legal?"

"One hundred percent," Nash said. "It's no different than her using mace, except for the fact it's a little more forceful and a lot more persuasive. In fact, I have one myself. You should try it before passing judgment."

Sherry took the PPD and turned it over in her hand. "I'll need to practice using it."

"We have plenty of room at the farm for you to fire off a few rounds," Nash said.

Jo relented. "I do like the idea of Sherry having some protection but would feel better knowing she was comfortable handling it."

"Then, it's settled." Nash glanced at his watch. "I need to get back to work."

Sherry walked them to the door. "Thanks for the food, the towels and the personal protection device. I promise I'll keep it safely tucked away in my drawer until I can practice using it."

Nash waited until they had left and were on the road to apologize. "I'm sorry about the surprise. I wasn't sure you would approve, so I figured it was best for you to see it in person to convince you it was safe for Sherry."

"I probably would've been dead-set against it," Jo admitted. "But now that I've seen it, I think it will be good for her to have some sort of protection. I am happy to hear she has a neighbor."

They reached the farm, and Nash parked near the barn. "I'll see you at dinner?"

"Yes, dinner. Delta's whipping up one of Gary's favorite meals – meatloaf, mashed potatoes and gravy along with fresh corn on the cob."

"I'm already hungry." Nash patted his stomach. "It sounds delicious. It's going to be an exciting evening."

"Exciting? I didn't know meatloaf and vegetables excited you," Jo teased.

"Are you kidding? It's one of my favorites too."

"Nash Greyson," Jo wagged her finger. "You are not excited about dinner."

"I...I am. Like I said, I'm already hungry."

Jo crossed her arms, growing suspicious at the expression on Nash's face. "Is there something you're not telling me?"

Nash gave her a quick peck on the cheek. He mumbled something about getting back to work so he would be done in time for dinner and then hustled into the workshop.

"Odd." Jo shook her head as she stared at the closed door before making her way across the parking lot to check on the mercantile and bakery.

The women were eager to hear about Sherry's apartment, and Jo promised to share details at dinner before returning to the house where she found Delta in the kitchen. "How's Sherry?"

"Good. She said to thank you for the food. She loved the embroidered towels. As far as the gun, she'll need some target practice."

"Gun?" Delta dropped the spoon she was holding. "You gave her a gun?"

"I didn't – Nash did. Technically, it's a personal protection device, not a gun." Jo briefly explained how the device worked.

"I, for one, think it's a good idea."

"After giving it some thought, I have to agree." Jo reached for an apron and slipped it over her head. "I'm here to help. What are you working on?"

"Dessert. Peanut butter truffles to be exact. We need to start rolling the balls."

Jo washed her hands and grabbed a handful of the chilled mixture. She rolled the balls and then dipped them in a bowl of melted chocolate before carefully placing them on wax paper.

After she finished, Delta placed the tray inside the fridge to cool. "Have you made a final decision on the new resident?"

"Not yet. I spoke with Pastor Murphy briefly before heading to Sherry's and promised to call him back when I got home." Jo untied her apron. "Her name is Laverne Huntsman. Does the name ring a bell?"

Delta, who had previously worked as a cook at the penitentiary, shook her head. "Nope. I would remember the name."

"She worked in the prison kitchen too, so I thought you might have met her." It had been a couple months since Jo had last accompanied Pastor Murphy to Central State Women's Penitentiary, where they visited a trio of women who were on track to be released soon.

Since her last visit, one of the women had contacted her family and was returning to another part of the state.

The second, who struck Jo as the most promising, became involved in an altercation with another inmate. The incident resulted in the board rescinding her early release. She would remain incarcerated and serve out the rest of her sentence behind bars.

The last, Laverne Huntsman, was the one Jo remembered best because of her in-your-face and over-the-top attitude. "She struck me as a little...overbearing."

"So, maybe she won't be a good fit." Levelheaded Delta had a heart of gold, but she never let her emotions cloud her judgment and decision making, something Jo struggled with.

"I'm leaning that way," Jo admitted. "I had better call him back." She left Delta in the kitchen and wandered into her office.

Jo reached for her cell phone and paused. The fifty-something woman would have trouble finding employment, particularly after potential employers discovered her time behind bars was a direct result of forgery and stealing from her previous employer. Where would she go?

Before she could change her mind, she dialed the pastor's cell phone. He answered on the first ring. "Hello, Joanna."

"Hello, Pastor Murphy. I thought I would get back with you to discuss Laverne Huntsman."

"Yes. Laverne." There was a muffled sound in the background, and the pastor sounded distracted. "I've been praying about this all day, that God would lead you to the right decision since you're Laverne's last hope."

"Last hope?" Jo echoed.

"The women's home in Kansas City was my backup plan in case you said 'no.' I contacted them a couple hours ago. The state filled their only vacancy with a charity case. The home is at capacity. There won't be another opening for six weeks. Laverne is being released the day after tomorrow."

"I...I don't know about her, Pastor." Jo removed a sheet of paper from the file folder she'd created after visiting Laverne at the women's prison. She slipped her reading glasses on. "I kept a copy of the list she gave us."

"Yes. Laverne's list. I forgot about that." There was a pause on the other end of the line. "Jo, I'm right around the corner from your place. Would it be possible for me to drop by so we could discuss the matter in person?"

"Yes, of course. Delta is fixing supper now."

Jo heard a small noise coming from the doorway. It was Delta. "I didn't mean to eavesdrop, but we have more than enough food. Pastor Murphy is welcome to join us."

"Delta said we have plenty of food. If you don't have plans, why don't you join us for dinner?"

"Are you sure? I don't mean to impose."

"It's no imposition at all," Jo assured him. "We're having meatloaf, mashed potatoes and gravy and corn on the cob."

The pastor chuckled. "You twisted my arm. There's no way I can pass up one of Delta's home-cooked meals."

"It's settled. We'll see you in a few minutes."

Delta waited for Jo to end the call. "The pastor's staying for supper?"

"He is. He said he can't pass up one of your home-cooked meals." Jo tossed the phone on the desk and repeated their brief conversation.

"The woman has nowhere to go," Delta said. "He's going to pressure you to take her in."

"I'm sure he will." Jo absentmindedly reached for the list of demands, her eyes scanning the sheet.

Delta plopped down in the chair opposite her. "What's that?"

"Laverne's list of demands." Jo handed her the sheet.

Delta made a snorting sound. "List of demands?" She squinted her eyes and read the list aloud:

Number one. Digital requirements. One hour of internet and one hour of uninterrupted television time per day. No exceptions.

Number two. Fragrance-free soaps and detergents available at all times. I have extremely sensitive skin and break out in hives.

"I got some lye in the cupboard," Delta joked.

"Delta," Jo gave her a stern look. "I'm not sure if I think that's unreasonable, but it probably isn't."

Delta continued:

Number three. Quiet time from nine p.m. until six a.m.

Number four. Organic fruits and vegetables available for consumption.

Number Five.

Delta's jaw dropped. "No way. I'm gonna tell you right now I have a real problem with number five."

Chapter 3

Jo chuckled. "I figured you would have a problem with Laverne's final demand."

Delta read number five on Laverne's list of demands. "Full access to the kitchen at all times to enhance my cooking creativity." She waved the list in the air. "Ain't no way – no how – this woman is having unlimited access to my kitchen."

She sprang from the chair. "I don't know who this woman thinks she is, going around demanding this and that. She should be begging to get in here. You're going to tell the Pastor 'no' to this nonsense, right?"

"That was my plan."

Before Delta could reply, the doorbell rang. "I'll get it. I'll set Pastor Murphy straight. We're gonna nip Laverne's hoity-toity demands in the bud." The look on Delta's face was thunderous as she marched out of the office.

Jo slid the paper back inside the folder and trailed behind, following the loud voices to the front porch.

Poor Pastor Murphy stood off to the side, his expression unreadable as Delta ranted and raved about Laverne.

"Who does this woman think she is?" Delta didn't wait for an answer, never gave the pastor a chance to respond as she wagged her finger at him. "She should be thanking her lucky stars that Jo would even consider letting her move to the farm. She's expecting a red-carpet rollout. I say she needs to find someone else to roll out the carpet for her."

The pastor lifted both hands. "I can see Laverne has ruffled your feathers. She does seem to have a bit of an..." He paused as if searching for the right words. "Ego. I've met with her several times. Without going into any of the details because of privacy issues, let me say I believe her quirks are a defense mechanism."

Jo joined them on the porch. "I feel awful about her not having somewhere to go, but I don't see her being a good fit for us."

The pastor's expression grew grim, and he briefly closed his eyes. "I understand. And to be completely honest, I can't blame you. She literally has nowhere to go. I even thought about letting her camp out in the back of the church for a couple days, until I can figure something else out."

Jo could almost feel the pastor's desperation. He worked tirelessly to help the women in the prison system. "You may want to have a conversation with her," she suggested. "Be blunt and level with her."

"I will. I have." He tapped the side of his forehead. "It doesn't seem to sink in. Whatever is in her head just comes out of her mouth. She insults and compliments in the same sentence."

"Jekyll and Hyde," Delta muttered.

"Is there anyone else coming up for release in the near future who might be a good fit for the farm?" There was one other concern nagging in the back of Jo's mind. To retain their tax-exempt status and to keep the doors open, she needed to maintain a seventy-five percent or higher resident occupancy rate.

With two open spots, it was only a matter of time before someone discovered she didn't meet the criteria. If the state stopped by for an unannounced inspection, she would be forced to shut down.

There were still a handful of Divine locals who were opposed to the farm. All it would take was one anonymous phone call to the right person. In other words, she needed to move fast to fill Sherry's vacancy. Filling both would be even better.

"I've left a message for the prison warden. As soon as I hear something, I'll let you know," Pastor Murphy promised.

The kitchen timer echoed through the porch's screen door. "My meatloaf is ready." Delta darted back inside, and the pastor waited until she was gone. "She's dead set against Laverne."

"It was her list of demands. The one where Laverne wanted unlimited access to the kitchen sent Delta over the top." Jo held the door for the pastor and motioned for him to come inside. "On a brighter note, Sherry has settled into her new apartment."

The pastor and Jo chatted about Sherry as the residents trickled in. Leah headed to the kitchen to help Delta while Raylene and Kelli began setting the table.

Nash arrived, followed by Gary and Leah, who were the last to join them.

"Sorry I didn't make it here in time to help set the table," Leah apologized. "Gary and I were working on the new side bed we tilled up today."

Delta appeared in the doorway, tapping the side of a small tin cup with a metal spoon. "Dinner is ready. Come and get it before it gets cold."

Jo poured the drinks, making her way around the table that felt oddly empty without Sherry. For the umpteenth time, she wondered how she was doing, if she was lonely and then wondered if she should've invited her to supper.

Delta followed behind Jo, placing baskets of bread in the center. "Are you missing Sherry?"

"Yeah." Jo swallowed hard as she stared at the empty chair. "Maybe we should've invited her to dinner."

"I already did, right before I stopped by your office. She thanked me, and politely declined."

"Did you tell her you were serving your famous meatloaf?" Jo teased.

"Yes, ma'am. She said to save her a piece."

The group took their places at the table. Nash prayed over the food, adding a special prayer for Sherry.

"Amen," Jo echoed, and then lifted her head. "Sherry is doing great. Nash and I stopped by her apartment earlier to deliver some furniture. She's looking forward to having company and showing off her place."

"When are we getting a new resident?" Raylene asked. "I thought you had a couple in mind."

"I did." Jo briefly explained one had become involved in an incident and was no longer eligible for early release, and the other was moving to another part of the state. "There was one more, but I've decided against her."

"Why?" Kelli asked.

"I have a few concerns."

Delta made an unhappy sound.

Nash grinned. "Looks like Delta has something to say."

"Darn tootin'," she muttered under her breath.

"Do you know who she is?" Raylene reached for a dinner roll.

"I never met the woman, and based on her list of demands, I don't want to."

"List of demands?" Leah's eyes grew wide.

Jo shifted, reluctant to discuss the woman, who wasn't there to defend herself.

Pastor Murphy cleared his throat. "Laverne isn't a bad person. In fact, she has a good heart."

"Laverne," Raylene repeated. "I knew a Laverne in prison. She worked in the kitchen. The lady was a trip."

"Laverne Huntsman?" Jo asked.

"That's her." Raylene nodded. "She was always getting into some sort of trouble. I'm surprised she's getting out of prison. I take that back, maybe they got tired of her and decided to let her out early."

Delta sawed off a slice of meatloaf. "We don't need any of that mess."

Halfway through the meal, Pastor Murphy excused himself to take an important call. He returned a short time later, a concerned expression on his face.

"Bad news?" Jo asked as he resumed his spot at the table.

"Sort of. I just spoke to the prison warden. There are no releases coming up. It looks like you're going to have two open spots for at least another month, until the next list of parolees is determined."

A sick feeling settled in the pit of Jo's stomach. She needed one more resident. Perhaps if she could keep a low profile, no one would notice she was two residents shy of a full house.

Jo picked at her food, thinking about Tara's abrupt departure before Christmas and how it had put her in a bind.

"You okay?" Nash leaned in and whispered in her ear.

"Yes. No." Jo forced a smile. "I hope so."

After dinner, the women made quick work of clearing the table while Delta carried in the plate of decadent chocolate treats. "I'm trying something new," she announced. "These are peanut butter cream cheese truffle balls, served best with a side of vanilla ice cream."

Jo made her rounds with a pot of fresh coffee as the group sampled the sweet treat. She caught Nash giving Gary several funny looks.

Finally, she spoke. "Is there something going on? You and Gary keep giving each other secret signals."

Nash shook his head while Gary averted his gaze, looking even more uncomfortable than Nash. And guilty.

"Gary?" Jo arched a brow and pinned him with a stare.

He shook his head and slid down in his chair.

"Did you swallow wrong? I think he's choking on my truffle." Delta threw her dinner napkin on the table. She raced to the other side of the room and began pounding on his back. "Do you need some water?"

Gary shook his head as Delta continued pounding on his back.

"Maybe he needs the Heimlich maneuver," Jo said.

"Right." Delta dragged Gary from his chair. She wrapped her ample arms around his abdomen and squeezed. "We're gonna dislodge that truffle. Hang on."

"Delta," he grunted. "Please stop."

"Did we get it?" Delta loosened her grip.

Gary lowered to one knee.

"He's going down!" Delta shouted. "Call 911!"

36

"Don't call 911." Gary calmly reached into his front pocket. "I didn't want to have to do this right here, right now, but you always were an unconventional woman. I guess this shouldn't be any different."

Jo clasped her hands as it dawned on her what was happening.

Chapter 4

Gary removed a small jewelry box from his pants pocket. "Delta Childress, will you marry me?"

"M...marry?" Delta pressed a hand to her chest and began to sway. "You mean you weren't choking?"

"No. I was contemplating how I was gonna pull off a romantic proposal. But you kinda decided it for me." Gary held up the box and repeated his question. "I'm too old to be down here on my knee much longer. You gonna get hitched to me or not?"

"Of course," Delta gasped. "Of course, I'll marry you."

Gary's hand trembled as he removed the diamond engagement ring from the holder and carefully placed it on Delta's finger.

"It's beautiful," she said breathlessly. "I do. I mean...I will. When?"

"First, I gotta get up." Gary grabbed hold of the edge of the chair and pulled himself to his feet. "We can get hitched just as soon as you like."

"Congratulations. It couldn't have happened to a finer couple. I would be honored to officiate," Pastor Murphy offered.

Delta tilted her hand as she admired the ring. "I've never been proposed to. Well, maybe once but it was from Clovis Ramblich. Good thing I didn't accept. He ended up beating his wife."

"I remember Clovis," Gary said. "He was a bad man."

While the group gathered around Gary and Delta, hugging and congratulating them, Jo slipped into the kitchen to grab some glasses and sparkling cider.

Nash trailed behind. "Can I help?"

"Sure." Jo handed him an empty tray. "You knew Gary planned to propose."

"I did." Nash cast a quick glance over his shoulder. "He's had the ring for nearly a week, carrying it around in his pocket. He almost chickened out tonight until I threatened to spill the beans to you."

Jo smiled as the excited voices echoed from the dining room. "I think it's wonderful."

"Me too. They deserve to be happy." Nash waited for Jo to fill the glasses and began placing them on the tray. "Delta will keep Gary on his toes, that's for sure."

Jo filled the last two glasses, and then they carried them into the dining room where they began passing them out. She handed the last glass to the pastor. "I propose a toast – to Delta and Gary, may you have many years of wedded bliss."

"To wedded bliss." Delta downed her cider. "We were just talking. Would it be all right to have the wedding here at the farm?"

"All right? I think it would be perfect," Jo gave them both a quick hug and then returned to the kitchen. She pulled her cell phone from her pocket and dialed Sherry's number.

Sherry picked up on the first ring. "Hi, Jo."

"Hi, Sherry. How are you doing?"

"Oh...kay."

Jo's radar immediately went up at the uncertainty in Sherry's voice. "What's going on?"

"I took some trash to the dumpster downstairs and thought I saw someone hanging around."

Jo glanced at the clock. The hardware store had closed at six, more than half an hour earlier. "It could be someone from the hardware store, closing up for the night. Are you inside your apartment now?"

"I am. The doors are locked. Hang on." There was a long moment of silence. "I can see the lights on over at your brother's theater from my living room window."

"Miles has been putting in long hours, trying to get the place ready to open in a few weeks. Would you like me to have him stop by and have a look around?"

"I...if you don't mind."

Delta burst into the kitchen; her face flushed. "Is that Sherry?"

"It is." Jo covered the mouthpiece. "I haven't said anything yet."

"Don't," Delta shook her head. "Gary and I want to run over there and tell her in person."

"Yes. Of course." Jo returned to the call. "Never mind. Gary, Delta and I are on our way over. We're leaving now."

"Thanks, Jo."

Jo ended the call. "Sherry said she thinks someone was hanging around the dumpster out back."

"Oh, dear. Well, maybe it's a good thing we're going over there." Delta stuck her head inside the dining room. "C'mon, Gary," she hollered. "We're going to visit Sherry."

Gary appeared in the doorway. "And leave our impromptu party?"

"Everyone stay put," Delta ordered. "We're making a quick trip to town to give Sherry the good news in person. We shouldn't be more than half an hour."

"I'm sorry, Delta, I need to get going." Pastor Murphy followed Nash into the kitchen. "I have an evening appointment. Thanks for dinner. Congratulations on the engagement. Let me know when you've picked a date."

The residents, led by Raylene, gathered in the kitchen. "We're heading home too."

Delta looked deflated. "Everyone's leaving? I thought we could celebrate."

"We're going to celebrate." Jo patted her arm. "In fact, I think we should have an official engagement party this weekend. We can invite Marlee, Claire, your niece, along with some other friends and make it a real party."

Delta brightened. "I like that idea."

"In the meantime, Sherry is expecting us." Jo turned to Nash. "Would you like to tag along?"

"Unfortunately, I have some cleaning up to do in the workshop." Nash gave Jo a peck on the cheek and followed the women out the back door.

Jo grabbed the keys off the hook and watched a bolt of brown flash past. Duke, the family hound dog, stood patiently waiting for her at the bottom of the steps.

She started to shoo him back inside and then changed her mind. "C'mon, Duke. We're going for a ride."

"We're gonna follow you in Gary's truck," Delta said.

"Sounds good." Jo, who was the first to arrive, parked behind the hardware store, and she and Duke exited the vehicle, watching as Gary's truck pulled in next to her.

Delta sprang from the vehicle and slammed the door. "We decided on a summer wedding at the farm. The ceremony will be on the front porch with Pastor Murphy officiating. We're thinking about hiring Marlee to cater the reception."

"It sounds wonderful. I love it." Jo grabbed Duke's leash and led the way up the stairs to the apartment's main entrance. The door leading to the shared hallway was locked.

Jo tapped out a text, and Sherry appeared moments later. "That was fast." She patted Duke on the head. "You brought Duke."

"I figured he could take a look around while we're here." Jo and Duke shifted to the side to wait for Gary and Delta to join them.

"We're getting married," Delta sing-songed as she thrust her hand in the air, displaying the glittering diamond. "Gary proposed."

"You did? Congratulations," Sherry clapped her hands. "I figured it was only a matter of time."

"We're getting married at the farm this summer. I want you and the other women to be my bridesmaids."

"A bridesmaid? I've never been one before."

"And I've never been a bride, so we're all newbies at this wedding jazz."

"A beautiful bride and beautiful bridesmaids," Jo said. "I can hardly wait."

Delta tapped Jo's arm. "Will you be my maid of honor?"

"I would be honored," Jo said sincerely.

Sherry led the couple inside to show them around while Jo lingered in the hallway, studying the other apartment doors. She could hear the thump of music echoing from the unit to the right.

Duke let out a low whine, his signal he needed to go out. "Hang on." Jo hurried to Sherry's door and stuck her head inside. "Duke and I are taking a quick trip out. We'll be back in a few minutes."

Sherry gave her a thumbs up. "Be careful."

Duke scrambled down the steps. He took care of business first, and then Jo led him around the side of the building. He stopped several times along the way to investigate before they reached the sidewalk out front.

Jo noticed a beam of light coming from the old movie theater several yards away. She tugged on Duke's leash. "Let's say hello to Miles."

The theater's front door was ajar, and Jo eased it open. "Miles? Are you in here?"

Jo's half-brother appeared. "Hey, Jo. What brings you to this part of town at this hour?"

"Duke and I are visiting my former resident, Sherry, and thought we would stop by." Jo briefly explained Sherry had moved into an apartment above the hardware store and had noticed someone lurking about.

"There are a lot of early evening walkers. I see people all of the time."

"Now that the weather is getting warmer, I'm sure that's true." Jo changed the subject. "How are your renovations going?"

Miles had recently purchased the old theater, using the money he'd gotten from Jo's settlement when it was determined he was her half-brother. It had been a rocky beginning – to say the least – but after giving it some thought and with apologies on both sides, the two were working hard to build a relationship.

Part of Jo's uneasiness was Miles' desire to stay in Divine and put down roots. She was against it until he explained that after his mother's death, he had no family. Jo was the only family he had left.

He'd convinced her he had big plans for the old theater and wanted to convert it into a dine-in movie theater. She could hear the excitement in his voice when he talked about it. Despite his excitement and what seemed like a reasonable reason for remaining in Divine, there was still an inkling of wariness when it came to Miles Parker.

He'd suddenly – and abruptly – left town on more than one occasion, always claiming a "business matter" had cropped up. She'd questioned him about it, and, at best, his answers were evasive.

When Jo really thought about it, she realized she knew very little about her half-brother. Her gut told her there was more to Miles' business matters than he let on – something he was determined to keep a secret.

"It's going great. The renovations are moving right along. I should have the place ready for a soft opening in about a month. My plan is to invite some of the local officials, not to mention the media, to tour the place and help me get the word out."

"It sounds as if you have a solid plan."

Miles showed her around the lobby, and Jo was impressed by his progress. She was thrilled to see he'd retained the natural charm of the original theater and complimented him on it.

She consulted her watch. "I had better get back to Sherry's place. She's going to wonder what happened to me."

Miles followed her out of the building. "I'm sure it's going to take some time for her to get used to living alone. I'll keep an eye out for her if you want when I'm around."

"Thanks. That would be great." Jo tightened her grip on Duke's leash as he attempted to pull away.

He let out a warning growl as a man rounded the corner, nearly colliding with her.

She took a quick step back, and Duke growled again.

"Duke." Jo placed a firm hand on his side as she eyed the man. "Hello."

"Hello."

"Chet, there you are," Miles said. "I thought you weren't gonna show. I was getting ready to close up shop and head back to the campground."

"Sorry," the man said. "I got held up running a couple errands, and it set me back."

"Chet, this is my sister, Jo Pepperdine. Jo, this is Chet Cleaper. He's the head maintenance guy out at the campground where I'm staying."

Jo offered the man a polite smile as he stared at her, and she got the uneasy feeling he was sizing her up. "Joanna Pepperdine, the loaded lady who houses the..." Chet abruptly stopped.

"I run a farm for women who are trying to get back on their feet." Jo turned to her brother. "I should get going. I'll see you later."

"Sure thing, Jo. And about the other, I'll swing by the hardware store on my way out before heading home tonight."

"Thanks." Jo smiled at both men and led Duke to the edge of the sidewalk. Her scalp tingled, and she didn't have to turn around to know the man was watching her.

Chapter 5

Jo returned to find Sherry, Gary and Delta waiting for her in the parking lot.

"We were getting ready to set up a search party," Delta joked. "What happened to you?"

"Duke and I went for a walk. I noticed the lights were on over at Miles' theater and stopped by to chat with him for a minute."

"He's got the place looking good. I walked by there earlier and caught a glimpse of the inside. It looks cool." Sherry let out a yawn and quickly covered her mouth. "Excuse me. I didn't mean to do that."

"We best get going so you can get ready for bed," Delta said. "I think we've all had enough excitement for one day."

Jo gave Sherry a quick hug while Delta and Gary returned to the truck. "Promise me you'll call if you need anything at all."

"I will. Thanks, Jo. Thanks for everything."

"You're welcome. Have you met your neighbor?"

"Not yet. It's a guy. I've heard him slam his door a couple times and caught a glimpse of him leaving yesterday."

"Perhaps he was the one down by the dumpster."

"Could be. And could be I'm just being paranoid." Sherry started to say something else and then stopped.

"What is it?"

"I get the feeling sometimes that someone is watching me."

Jo knew exactly what she meant and had gotten the same feeling from Chet Cleaper. She wondered how well Miles knew his "handyman." "Just be careful and aware of your surroundings."

"Will do." Sherry returned upstairs while Jo coaxed Duke into the cab of the truck. She motioned to Gary, who rolled down his driver's side window.

"Everything okay?" Delta asked.

"I hope so. When Duke and I stopped by Miles' place, a friend of his showed up. Have you ever met Chet Cleaper? He works at the campground where Miles is staying."

"Chet Cleaper," Gary repeated. "Mighta heard the name a time or two."

"He hit your radar," Delta guessed.

"He did. He hit Duke's radar too."

"Duke's got a keen sense for bad people," Delta said. "Do you think he may be the one hanging around here?"

"I don't know. It could be Sherry's become more aware of her surroundings now that she's on her own and living alone." Jo told them she'd see them back at the farm and hopped into the truck.

Gary and Delta arrived home first and parked near the front porch.

Jo wasn't far behind and grinned as she watched Gary reach for Delta's hand as they strolled across the driveway. She could hear the tinkle of Delta's laughter as it filled the evening air.

"A match made in heaven," she whispered under her breath. She was still smiling as she slipped inside the workshop.

Nash stood near the bench in the back. "Hey, Jo. How's Sherry?"

"Okay." Jo leaned her hip against the door. "She said she thought someone was hanging around outside." Jo told him how Duke and she had patrolled the area, stopped at the theater to talk to Miles and met Chet. "Have you ever heard of Chet Cleaper?"

"No. Why?"

"He gave me a weird feeling, like he was sizing me up. When I left, I'm almost sure he was watching me."

"And you think he might be watching Sherry?"

"I don't know." Jo shoved her hands in her pockets. "I hope not."

Nash set the sander on the table and crossed the room. He pulled her into his arms and placed a light kiss on the top of her head. "That's what I love about you. You care." He tightened his grip, and Jo's heart skipped a beat as she breathed in his masculine scent, a mixture of sawdust and aftershave. "You smell nice."

Nash chuckled, and Jo could feel the laughter on her cheek as it rumbled through his chest. "Like an old farm workshop."

"What's wrong with that?" Jo demanded as she lifted her head. "I happen to like it."

"There's nothing wrong with it." Nash ran a light hand down her cheek and then tilted her chin as he lowered his head. His lips lightly brushed against hers. She leaned in, and the kiss deepened.

Jo wrapped her arms around Nash's neck and abandoned herself to the kiss. Finally, he took a step back. Jo's cheeks were flushed, and her breathing uneven. She said the first thing that popped into her head. "It's getting hot in here."

"Yes, it is." Nash's eyes smoldered. "We better watch it, or we'll end up setting this place on fire," he teased.

Jo pressed a light hand to her cheek. "And on that note, I had better get going."

Nash followed her to the door. The porch light was on, and Jo could see Gary and Delta on the porch swing. Duke was wedged between them, his head in Delta's lap, and his tail thumping contentedly against Gary's leg.

"I guess this means Delta will be moving out," Nash said.

The thought hadn't occurred to Jo, but Nash was right. Delta would be moving in with Gary after the wedding. "Hopefully, she'll want to keep working for me."

"I don't see why not. The only thing that will change is where she lays her head at night," Nash joked. "This place is emptying out fast. Speaking of emptying out, what are you going to do about the open spots?"

"I don't know. I need to fill them, but there's only one potential tenant, Laverne, the one I mentioned at dinner, and she sounds challenging."

"I've never known you to back down from a challenge," Nash teased. "You sure you don't want to reconsider? Can this woman really be that bad?"

Jo frowned. "First impressions are sometimes deceiving. Delta was dead set against it when she found out one of the woman's demands is to have full access to the kitchen."

"Give her full access to the common area kitchenette. Lay down the rules that the main kitchen is Delta's domain."

"That's a great idea and a good compromise." Jo rubbed a weary hand across her brow. "Maybe I'll sleep on it."

"I think that's a wise decision." Nash gave her a gentle kiss. "Now, get going before I change my mind about heating this place up."

Chapter 6

It was a restless night for Jo. She tossed and turned, worrying about her open spots. She wondered if her plan to help former female convicts was losing steam. What if no one wanted to come to the farm?

She thought about her troubled former resident, Tara, who had run off to Chicago to see her daughter during the holidays. Could Tara, who was now back in prison, be bad-mouthing Jo and the home to anyone who would listen?

Would Pastor Murphy tell her if that was the case? She thought about Chet Cleaper. Something about the man hit Jo's radar, the way he looked at her. What if Miles had mentioned Sherry to him and he was watching her?

Finally, she fell into a fitful sleep. When she woke, it was still dark. She rolled over to check the bedside clock – five twenty-five. She groaned as she pulled the covers over her head.

Jo began working on a mental list of people she planned to invite to the engagement party. Finally, she threw the covers off and crawled out of bed.

She flipped the bathroom light on and stared at the bloodshot eyes of the woman in the mirror. Gray roots were popping out everywhere, and a new wrinkle had carved a path between her eyebrows.

Jo pulled on the corners of her mouth, creating a ghostly grimace that made her laugh. Forcing herself to stop nitpicking, she hurried through her morning routine. After finishing, she headed down the hall before changing her mind and doing an about-face.

It had been days since she'd spent quiet time in her recently renovated book nook. She reached the top of the stairs and fumbled for the light switch, breathing in the vanilla smell of old books.

Jo reached for her Bible and sank down in her worn leather armchair, savoring the comfortable quietness of her sanctuary. She breathed deeply before removing the bookmark and slipping her reading glasses on.

She read through several chapters until she got to a Bible verse that struck a chord. Jo read it a second time:

"You did not choose me, but I chose you and appointed you that you should go and bear fruit and that your fruit should abide, so that whatever you ask the Father in my name, he may give it to you." John 15:16

Jo bowed her head and prayed for peace. She asked God to protect Sherry, and that he would reveal to her anything she should be concerned about. She prayed for Delta and Gary, thanking him for bringing them together. She prayed for the residents, and last but not least, she asked God to give her a clear sign of what to do about her two open spots.

A sense of peace filled Jo as she closed her Bible. She placed it on the table, running a light hand over the top. God had gotten her this far. He wasn't about to leave her high and dry now.

"Your way, not mine," Jo whispered as she eased out of the chair. She gave the Bible one final look before making her way downstairs.

The comforting aroma of cinnamon and baked bread filled the kitchen. Delta stood at the counter, her back to the door, belting out a tune at the top of her lungs.

"Delta's goin' to the chapel, and she's gonna marry Gary. Goin' to the chapel..."

"Don't you mean goin' to the front porch?" Jo laughed.

Delta spun around. "Joanna Pepperdine. You should know better than to sneak up on an old lady," she scolded.

"First of all, you're not old, and second of all, I wasn't sneaking. You wouldn't have heard a herd of elephants coming with all of the racket you're making." Jo crossed the kitchen and peered into Delta's mixing bowl. "What are you making?"

"Delta's divine gooey cinnamon muffins. They're for the bakeshop. I just took a batch out of the oven." She pointed to the top of the stove. "You should try one."

"Only if you'll join me," Jo bargained.

"I would love to." Delta rinsed her hands in the sink and reached for the kitchen towel. "You're up before the rooster crowed this morning."

"It was a restless night." Jo plucked two muffins from a tin and carried them to the table while Delta refilled her coffee cup and poured a fresh one for Jo.

"I wasn't sleeping well myself. I finally gave up and decided to get a head start on the day." Delta set the cups on the table before settling in. "I have a lot on my mind."

"About the wedding?" Jo blew on the hot coffee and took a tentative sip. "You aren't getting cold feet, are you?"

"Not cold feet. Just worried about leaving the farm."

"You're not leaving, leaving, as in putting in your notice?"

"Nah." Delta waved dismissively. "I meant moving into Gary's place and leaving you rambling around this big old farmhouse all by yourself."

Jo pointed to Duke, who was sprawled out on the kitchen floor. "I'll still have Duke. And Nash and the women are right next door."

"I suppose. Maybe I'm trying to work it all out since everything is happening so fast." Delta peeled off the muffin wrapper and took a big bite. "Mmm. Mmm. I am a marvelous baker if I do say so myself."

"The best." Jo joined her friend, taking a big bite of the muffin. The top was crunchy cinnamon, the muffin was fluffy and light, and there was a surprise in the center. "There's a treat in the middle. Cinnamon and sugar along with something else."

Delta grinned. "Ten bucks if you can tell me what it is."

"Cream cheese," Jo guessed.

"I don't have ten bucks on me, but you would be right on."

Jo polished off the rest of the muffin. "These are delish," she mumbled. "My goodness. I could eat at least two more."

"We gotta save some for the bakeshop. Have you had a chance to run last week's sales numbers yet?"

"They were down again for the third straight week in a row." Although the mercantile was doing a brisk business, the bakeshop sales were lagging. Jo hadn't delved into it yet, to try to figure out why sales were down. It was one more concern to add to all her others.

"I'm still trying to figure out why. In the meantime, let me help." Jo donned an apron, washed her hands and joined her friend at the counter. They finished whipping up another batch of the delicious muffins and filled the oven with another round of trays.

The back door slammed, and Raylene appeared. "I'm here to report for duty."

Delta did a double-take, taking in the dark circles under the woman's eyes. "You look like you should be reporting for bed."

"It was a rough night."

"You miss Sherry," Jo guessed. Sherry and Raylene were close, closer than any of the other residents.

"Yes, and I'm worried about her. She sent me an email last night. She said someone was hanging around outside."

"I heard the same." Jo's expression grew grim. "I wonder if she had another incident or was telling you about the one she told me about."

"This was around eleven, so I doubt it was the same. We chatted back and forth on Facebook, and then finally, she said she thought whoever it was, was gone."

"I need to run a few errands in town this morning. Maybe I'll check on her while I'm out." Jo handed her apron to Raylene and made a beeline for her office to grab her keys.

Raylene trailed behind. "Sherry is working early this morning."

"Then I won't have any trouble finding her."

"Why don't you have Raylene go with you." Delta joined them. "I have the kitchen under control."

"If you're sure."

"Yes, ma'am," Delta nodded.

"We shouldn't be long."

69

Their first stop was the post office. Jo ran inside to mail several packages while Raylene waited in the SUV. After finishing, Jo drove to the other side of town and parked in front of the deli.

She stepped onto the sidewalk and studied the apartment building directly across the street. Sherry's unit and her living room were in the front and on the left.

Her eyes drifted along the sidewalk. Miles' theater was mere steps away. If someone were standing near the edge of the sidewalk, they would have a partial view of Sherry's living room window.

Raylene joined Jo and followed her gaze. "Anyone standing over here could see into Sherry's apartment."

"Yes, they could. She has blinds. I'm sure she keeps them closed, especially at night, but anyone paying attention could easily tell if the lights were on and Sherry was home."

The deli hadn't yet opened, so Jo led the way around back. She gave the door leading to the kitchen a light rap, before calling out. "Hello? Marlee? Sherry?"

Sherry popped into view. "Hi, Jo, Raylene." She swung the door open and motioned for them to come inside. "What are you doing here?"

"Raylene told me about your online conversation last night, how you thought someone was out front watching your apartment," Jo said. "You should've called me."

"I didn't want to worry you."

Marlee, who was on the other side of the kitchen, made her way over. "What's this?"

Sherry shifted her feet. "I thought someone was lurking around last night and then watching from across the street. I also heard some noises outside my door. I checked the peephole before opening it but didn't see anything. Well...I take that back. I caught a glimpse of my neighbor whom I haven't met yet."

"You haven't met Todd Gilmore? He's a nice man, a little on the quiet side, though. He came in here the other day and introduced himself."

"I'm sorry to interrupt, but I was wondering if I could use the bathroom," Raylene said.

"Sure," Marlee motioned to Sherry. "She can use the one here in the back. Can you show her where it is?"

Sherry nodded and then led Raylene out of the kitchen.

Marlee waited until they were gone. "This is the first Sherry's mentioned someone lurking around, although I have noticed she's seemed a little on edge the last couple days."

Jo cast an anxious glance in their direction. "I wouldn't mind having a look around her unit, to see exactly what she's talking about, and her view." *And the view from Miles' theater*, she silently added.

"That's probably not a bad idea."

Jo waited for Sherry and Raylene to return. "I was telling Marlee that I would like to have a look around your apartment, for my own peace of mind, and to get a better idea of what exactly someone who's standing outside can see if they're watching your unit."

"Sure." Sherry reached into her pocket and pulled out a set of keys. "The gold one with the sticker opens the exterior door. The other one is for my unit. The little one is for my mailbox."

"This shouldn't take long." Jo, accompanied by Raylene, took a shortcut through the alleys to the building across the street. They climbed the stairs and unlocked the entrance door.

The women passed by the other occupied unit, and Jo could hear a loud banging. "Do you hear that?"

"Maybe whoever it is, is still moving in," Raylene whispered.

"Could be."

Boom. The floor shook.

"It sounds like something big just went down."
Jo sucked in a breath and gave the door a firm rap.

It grew quiet.

"Someone is in there," Raylene muttered under
her breath.

"There most certainly is." Jo pursed her lips and
rapped again, this time harder. "Hello? Anyone
home?" she hollered.

There was a thud, followed by silence.

"We know someone is in there. We can hear
you," Jo said in a loud voice.

The door flew open, and a tall, thin man with
blond hair appeared. "Do you know what time it
is?"

"It's early," Jo said.

"I was sleeping."

"With all of that banging going on? You must be Todd Gilmore." Jo held out her hand. "I'm Joanna Pepperdine, a local business owner and your neighbor, Sherry Marshall's, former landlord."

The man hesitated before taking Jo's hand. "Hello."

"Sherry said someone was lurking around last night, and we were wondering if you might have seen or heard anything."

"Lurking?" He shook his head. "No, although I didn't leave my apartment all evening."

"She's concerned someone is watching this building."

Todd shrugged his shoulders. "I'm sorry. I haven't noticed anything or anyone."

Jo relaxed her stance. "I think Sherry would feel more comfortable if you two were able to meet."

"Yes. Yes. I've been holed up in my apartment trying to beat a deadline. By the time I catch a breather, it's late in the evening. I'll be sure to stop by and introduce myself."

While he talked, Jo craned her neck, attempting to catch a glimpse of the inside of the man's apartment.

He must have realized what she was doing and abruptly shifted, blocking her view. "Is there anything else?"

"No, that's all," Jo said.

"I need to get back to work." He mumbled a good-bye and quickly closed the door.

"Hmm." Jo stared at the door and then continued down the hall to Sherry's unit.

"How can he be doing two things at the same time?" Raylene whispered as she followed Jo. "First, he tells us he was sleeping, and then he tells us he has to get back to work. Which was it?"

"Your guess is as good as mine." Jo opened Sherry's apartment door and waited for Raylene to join her. "He didn't hit my suspicious character radar, but he's definitely an odd duck."

"Same here." Raylene made her way across the living room to the windows. "Check this out. Anyone standing on the other side of the street has an unobstructed view of Sherry's living room."

Jo joined her. "Yes, they do." She inspected the cheap, plastic blinds. "These aren't the best for privacy. Maybe Sherry should add a layer of curtains."

"I was thinking the same thing."

The women slowly made their way around the apartment, checking the windows to make sure they were locked. Satisfied, Jo finished her inspection and waited for Raylene, who was in the bedroom.

She emerged, holding the PPD Nash had given Sherry. "Sherry has a weapon."

"It's an air gun," Jo said. "Nash gave it to her as a housewarming gift."

"An air gun?" Raylene turned it over in her hand. "You could've fooled me. This looks like the real deal."

"I wasn't on board with it until Nash explained how it works. It shoots hard, plastic mini-missiles or pepper spray rounds."

Raylene ran a light hand over the top. "I'll need one of these when I move out."

"I'm sure Nash will gift you one too." After Raylene returned the PPD to Sherry's bedroom, Jo locked the door behind them and then double-checked it before exiting the apartment.

She paused when they reached the bottom of the stairs and noticed a set of metal mailboxes attached to the wall.

The first one was labeled "Tool Time Hardware." The other three were numbered.

"I didn't notice these on the way up," Raylene said. "I wonder which one belongs to Sherry."

"I don't know." Jo leaned in for a closer inspection and realized there was something different about one of the mailboxes.

Chapter 7

There was a gouge along the side of the mailbox, as if someone had tried prying it open. Jo did a slow scan of their surroundings. The mailboxes were semi-secluded, hidden by the stairs.

"I wonder if this is Sherry's mailbox," Raylene said.

"We'll soon find out." Jo slipped Sherry's mail key in the slot, and the box opened.

On the inside and near the front was a white sticker with Sherry's name on it. "This is definitely her mailbox. There's something inside." Jo removed an envelope. It was a piece of mail addressed to Nicole Brewster.

"Wait here. I'm going to go get Sherry." Jo returned to the deli and found her working at the prep counter. "I want to show you something."

Sherry placed the spoon on the counter and followed Jo to the mailboxes.

"Your mailbox is damaged."

Sherry's eyes widened as she stared at it. "It wasn't like that when I checked my mail yesterday."

The back door flew open, and Wayne Malton joined them. "I thought I heard voices. Morning, Jo, Sherry. What's going on?"

"Sherry's mailbox is damaged. We found someone else's mail inside." Jo handed Wayne the envelope.

"This isn't a tenant of mine. Wait a minute..." Wayne tapped the top of the envelope. "Nicole filled out an application for one of the apartments. Why would she have her mail sent here?"

"Because she was certain she was moving in?"

Wayne leaned in for a closer inspection. "I'll reinforce all of the boxes this morning. It won't happen again," he promised before returning inside.

After he left, the trio returned to the deli where Marlee was waiting for them in the kitchen. "What happened?"

"Someone was tampering with Sherry's mailbox. Wayne happened to come out while we were looking at it and plans to reinforce all of them." Jo told Marlee that Sherry's mailbox was the only one that was damaged.

Marlee's eyes widened. "Tampering with mail or mailboxes is a federal offense."

"They weren't able to open it, so thankfully, nothing was taken," Jo said. "On a more positive note, Gary and Delta got engaged last night."

"I knew it." Marlee waved her spoon at Jo. "I figured it would happen sooner rather than later. When's the big day?"

"Sometime this summer. They haven't given me the exact date yet." Jo told her friend she was planning an engagement party for Sunday afternoon and invited her.

"Count me in."

Jo told her she would be sending an Evite via email, and then she and Raylene headed out. "While we're in town, I wouldn't mind stopping by Claire's place to tell her the good news."

Claire Harcourt owned Claire's Coin Laundromat. Her antique shop, Claire's Collectibles and Antiques, was right next door. The antique store wasn't open, but the twenty-four-hour laundromat was.

Through the big picture window, Jo caught a glimpse of her friend standing behind the counter.

Claire looked up as the door's bell jingled, announcing their arrival. "Joanna Pepperdine. I heard you got a little excitement going on at the farm."

"Excitement?"

"Gary proposed to Delta. I never pegged Delta as the marrying kind, but then she and Gary are two peas in a pod."

"And I thought I was going to be the one to share the good news."

"Carrie Ford told me. She said she heard it from Clyde over at the gas station. Gary was in there first thing this morning, filling up some gas cans. From what I was told, Gary's on Cloud Nine."

"They both are," Jo said. "I'm hosting an engagement party this Sunday afternoon and will be sending you an Evite since it's such short notice."

"I wouldn't miss it for the world. Is Delta gonna keep working for you?"

"Yes, at least that's the plan."

"Sherry waited on me at the deli yesterday. She told me all about her new apartment." Claire leaned her elbow on the counter. "I left a little extra for her tip to put toward some of her expenses. You must be very proud of that young woman."

"I am," Jo beamed. "I'm proud of all of the women."

Claire sobered. "It's such a shame there are a few jerks in this town who can't be happy for Sherry."

"What do you mean?" Jo asked the question but suspected she already knew exactly what Claire meant. Not everyone in the small town of Divine was thrilled with Jo's farm – or the farm's residents.

"Someone came in last night, complaining to one of my employees about the 'riff-raff' as she called it above the hardware store. I tried to find out who it was, but Sue didn't recognize the person. Said it was a woman. That's all I know."

Jo clenched her fists, a wave of sudden anger welling up inside her. "I wish I knew who it was. I would be sure to set them straight."

"You and me both." Claire cast Raylene a sideways glance. "Unfortunately, it looks like Sherry may have to work a little harder to prove herself. I'm confident it won't take long for the few holdouts to come to the conclusion that they're wrong. Maybe it's all for the best. They can see for themselves how Sherry has turned her life around and should be welcomed into our community with open arms."

"Claire is right. Maybe it's best to let Sherry prove they're wrong. Besides, you can't go around fighting all of Sherry's battles," Raylene said quietly.

"It still makes me furious."

"And rightly so." Claire brought up the farm. "You got a couple vacancies with Sherry moving out, not to mention that woman who ran off right before Christmas. It must feel a little empty around your place."

"It is, and you're right. I have some vacancies to fill," Jo blew air through thinned lips, once again thinking about her current dilemma, filling her with a sense of urgency. "The sooner, the better."

A customer arrived, and Jo told her friend good-bye before following Raylene out of the laundromat. "I have one more errand. I need to pick up some birdfeed at the hardware store. Delta said we're almost out."

"We can make as many stops as you want. I'm along for the ride," Raylene joked.

They entered the hardware store, which had just opened for the day. Wayne was in the back, standing behind the cash register.

It took a couple trips up and down the aisles before Jo tracked down the birdseed. She grabbed a big bag and carried it to the checkout.

Wayne watched as Jo slid it onto the counter. "I'm sorry about Sherry's mailbox. I'll have it taken care of before noon."

"Thanks, Wayne, I'm sure Sherry will appreciate it," Jo said.

"Heard you got some exciting news over at the farm. Gary finally popped the question, and he and Delta are getting hitched."

Jo shook her head in amazement. "I can't believe how fast news travels around this small town."

"Like wildfire," Wayne said. "Of course, once Carrie Ford gets ahold of something, you can't keep her quiet. She called Charlotte from the gas station as soon as Clyde told her."

"She's one busy woman. I'm hosting an engagement party this Sunday and will be sending you and Charlotte an Evite."

"We'll be there. That'll be thirteen forty-nine for the birdseed."

Jo swiped her card. "I better not forget to invite Carrie since she's the unofficial messenger."

Wayne laughed. "I can't wait to see what she creates for Gary and Delta for a wedding gift."

Carrie, a local taxidermist, took over the "family" business after the death of her last husband. During the Christmas season, she'd created two Santa's elves for the local kid's Christmas party Jo hosted at the farm.

The elves had scared several of the children, and Jo ended up stashing the evil-looking elves in a corner. She vowed if she hosted a children's party this year, she would somehow "misplace" the elves until after the holiday season ended.

"I can't wait to see what she comes up with, either. There's one thing for certain...it will be unique." Jo stashed her card in her wallet and reached for the bag of birdseed.

Wayne stopped her. "I'll carry this to the car."

"Thanks."

The trio trekked out of the store and to the SUV.

Jo popped the hatch, and Wayne placed the birdseed in the back bin. "Sherry seems to be settling in."

"She loves her new home. I'm so proud of her," Jo said.

"As you should be. She's a fine addition to our town." Wayne took a step back and wiped his hands on his jeans.

"Claire said not everyone is thrilled about Sherry moving into town. Have you heard anything?"

Wayne hesitated, and Jo could tell from the look on his face that he had.

"Someone complained to you about her."

"Yeah, but I don't pay them much mind."

"Who was it?"

Wayne shook his head. "I think it's best to let it go. It won't take long for Sherry to prove to the townsfolk they have nothing to fear." He patted Jo's shoulder. "You're a good woman, Joanna Pepperdine, better than most of the folks around here. You're doing the right thing. We all make mistakes, even the most self-righteous.

Unfortunately, Sherry made one that gives her a lot of unwanted attention. It'll be all right."

Raylene spoke. "Sherry called me last night to say she thought someone was watching the place."

"She did? I have surveillance cameras around the outside of the building, although they're mostly out front because of the store." Wayne tapped his chin thoughtfully. "Maybe I need to do a little tweaking to keep an eye on the alley entrance."

"It might not be a bad idea," Jo said.

"Don't worry, Jo. I'll do whatever is necessary to keep Sherry and my other tenant safe."

Jo thanked him and then climbed into the SUV, waiting for Raylene to join her.

"Wayne's a good guy."

"He is, and I feel better knowing he's aware that someone may be lurking around here."

Back at the farm, Raylene headed next door to start her shift at the mercantile. Jo placed the bag of birdseed by the back door and climbed the steps to the kitchen.

Delta was seated at the table, surrounded by recipe cards. "That didn't take long."

"We stopped by the post office and then the deli. Raylene and I decided to take a look around Sherry's apartment." Jo hung her keys on the hook by the door and sank into an empty chair. "Someone's been messing with her mailbox."

"Seriously?" Delta gave Jo her full attention. "Who would do such a thing?"

"Could be someone is trying to scare her." Jo told her what Claire and Wayne had said, that there were at least a couple disgruntled residents, voicing their opinions over Sherry's move into town.

"I wish I could find out who they were." Delta frowned. "I would track them down and give them a piece of my mind."

"Wayne seems to think it would only make matters worse. He's reinforcing the mailboxes and plans to change the settings on his surveillance cameras to keep a closer eye on the apartments." Jo changed the subject. "Half the town already knows about the engagement."

"Let me guess, Carrie Ford blabbed."

"Yep. Speaking of engagement, I'm going to head to the office to work on a list of people to send Evites to for Sunday's party. Is there anyone, in particular, you want to invite?"

"My niece, for sure. You can leave blabbermouth Carrie off the list. She's stealing my thunder."

"You can't leave Carrie off. She would be crushed."

"I suppose your right," Delta mumbled. "But seriously, the woman needs to learn to hold her tongue."

Jo grinned. "I can't wait to see what she gives you."

"What's that saying? Something old, something new. In Carrie's case, it will probably be something stuffed, something sewed..."

Jo picked up. "Something dead, something wed." She wandered into her office and settled in at the desk. While she waited for her computer to fire up, she began jotting down the names of people she planned to invite.

Once she logged in to her computer, her first task was to balance her personal and business bank accounts, and then she sorted through her emails. Her heart skipped a beat when she got to the bottom and saw one from the State of Kansas, Bureau of Licensing.

She double-clicked the message and scanned the official notification. Jo could feel the blood drain from her face when she read the last paragraph.

Chapter 8

Jo stared in disbelief as she read that her annual state inspection was only one week away. She scrambled to find her online calendar and searched for her upcoming appointments. There wasn't an entry for the annual state inspection.

She clicked through her folder of legal mumbo jumbo and paperwork she kept on the home, her licensing, the renewal and inspections. She scrolled the screen and found a notification from the previous month that she'd missed.

Jo opened the attachment. Sure enough, her annual inspection was scheduled for the following Monday morning at nine. Jo had exactly one week to find a new tenant. There was no way she would pass the state's inspection without a seventy-five percent occupancy rate.

Her hand shook as she printed off a copy of the notification. She snatched it off the printer and carried it into the kitchen. "I have less than a week to find a new resident."

"Huh?" Delta peered at her over the top of her reading glasses. "What are you talking about?"

Jo waved the piece of paper in the air. "The state's annual inspection is next Monday. Somehow, I missed it. I'm required to have at least seventy-five percent occupancy. If not, I won't pass the inspection and risk being shut down."

"Let me see that." Delta studied the notification. "Sure enough. You didn't know this was coming?"

"I overlooked it." Jo began to pace as a sense of panic set in. "What am I going to do?"

"Bring Sherry back for a week," Delta suggested.

"The state reviews each of the resident's progress reports. They'll see she's moved out."

"Call Pastor Murphy. Maybe someone has come up."

"Good idea." Jo pulled her cell phone from her pocket and tapped out a message to the pastor, asking him to call her.

"We can't freak out, at least not yet," Delta said. "We've been in worse messes than this."

"But not at the risk of being shut down." Jo began to feel light-headed. The state couldn't shut the doors. Where would the women go? What would happen to the farm? How long would it take to be reinstated?

Delta stepped in front of her. "Let's pray, not panic."

"Right." Jo nodded as she sucked in a breath. "You pray. I can't even form a coherent sentence right now."

The women bowed their heads. "Dear Lord. We're in a bind. We need your help. Jo needs a new resident right away. We know you have your hand on this place and have blessed the farm. We believe you're able to send the perfect person here to fill the vacancy within the next day or so. Thank you for answering our prayers."

"Amen," the women echoed in unison.

"Thanks, Delta. I'll go impatiently wait for Pastor Murphy's call." She returned to her office and carefully sorted through her emails to make sure she hadn't missed anything else. She had just finished the task when her cell phone rang.

"Pastor Murphy. Thank you for getting back with me so quickly." Jo got right to the point. "I need a new resident and fast," she said bluntly. "The state's annual inspection is next Monday. Seventy-five percent occupancy is required in order to pass the inspection."

"I see…" There was a long pause on the other end of the line. "I'm sorry, Jo. There isn't another parole hearing until the end of next week, and then a decision won't be made until after the hearing.

The only person who is still looking for a place to live is Laverne Huntsman."

Jo leaned back in her chair and closed her eyes. Was God trying to tell her to take Laverne? The woman needed a place to live. Jo needed a resident.

Scrambling to find a resident was unchartered territory. Jo had always been able to handpick each of the women, someone she felt would be a good fit for the farm.

Despite her best efforts, it hadn't always worked out. One example was Tara Cloyne, who, to her credit, hadn't been a troublemaker. She'd just up and left to sneak to Chicago to be with her daughter.

Pastor Murphy interrupted her musings. "If you don't take her in, she's going to be moving into the parsonage with me."

"Maybe you could loan her to me for a few days," Jo joked.

"Now, Jo, Laverne needs a permanent placement. It's not good for the women to bounce around. Once you take her, she's all yours."

"I don't like the way you said that."

"Maybe you need to give her another chance," the pastor suggested. "As I mentioned during our last visit, I believe a lot of Laverne's issues and her attitude are a defense mechanism. She strikes me as someone who's been burned. She may get to the farm and blossom into the person God meant for her to be. She needs someone to give her a chance."

A chance. Which is what Jo had given every other resident at the farm. Was Laverne any less worthy of the same opportunity? Having the same shot at making it outside the prison system? Perhaps this was God's way of telling Jo it wasn't up to her to pick and choose – it was up to him.

Delta and she had prayed about it. Maybe God was trying to tell her that Laverne *was* the right person for the farm.

"Ay-yi-yi."

"Many times, God's ways are not our own," the pastor said quietly.

"No. They're not. Can you give me a few minutes to think it over?"

"Of course. Laverne is being released at nine o'clock tomorrow morning. If you can't take her in, she'll be staying with me until I can find a home for her. If and when," he added.

Jo promised to call him back. She set her cell phone on the desk and drifted to the window. She wondered what was running through Laverne's mind, knowing she would be released from prison in less than twenty-four hours with nowhere to go.

It must be an awful feeling, believing no one in the world cared. No one other than Pastor Murphy, a stranger. The forgery and theft were concerning, but at least Laverne wasn't a killer, something Jo drew a hard line against.

She knew the women were given a small pittance on the day of their release in the form of a debit card. Attached to the debit card were steep fees, meaning the women were left with an even smaller amount, not nearly enough to survive on. They were also given clean clothes, donated by local thrift shops, including Jo's.

Her heart told her the right thing to do would be to take the woman in, but it wasn't just her she had to think about. There were the others on the farm...Leah, Kelli, Raylene and Michelle, not to mention Nash, Gary and Delta.

Her decision would affect all of them. Getting Laverne on the farm would be easy. Getting her out would be the hard part if it didn't work. This decision would have to be made with the long haul in mind.

Jo released a heavy sigh, feeling the weight of the farm, as well as the woman's future on her shoulders. If she put herself in Laverne's shoes, the decision was easy. It was when she hopped back into her own that the complications started piling up.

She briefly thought about talking it over with Delta but knew she was dead set against Laverne. She'd already said as much. Her main concern was Laverne's list of demands, which included access to Delta's kitchen.

The rules would have to be understood and agreed to before Laverne ever stepped foot on the farm if there was a chance of maintaining peace and tranquility on the home front.

Nash's words echoed in her head. Jo had never backed down from a challenge before. Now was not the time to start. She squared her shoulders and sucked in a breath. God had practically packed the woman's bags and parked her on the farm's doorstep.

He had seen her through some very rough times. A woman with a strong personality would be a piece of cake, at least that's what Jo told herself.

Before she could change her mind, she dialed Pastor Murphy's cell phone number.

"Hello, Jo."

"I've made a decision. Laverne can move here."

"Praise the Lord!" the pastor exploded. "I knew God was going to put her in your heart. I think there may be a period of adjustment all the way around, but I believe in the end, this was meant to be."

"Before you break out the bottle of bubbly, I want to meet with Laverne one more time, to lay down some ground rules before she sets foot on the farm."

"Yes. Sure. Of course. I completely understand." There was a shuffling on the other end of the line. "If we hurry, we can squeeze in a quick visit before visiting hours end. I'll have to call the prison and pull a few strings since we're not on the list of visitors."

"If you can't get us in there today, I can't take her tomorrow."

"Oh, I will," Pastor Murphy promised. "I'll call you right back."

Jo started to say something else and realized the pastor had already disconnected the call. Less than a minute later, the phone rang. "We're good to go. Would you like me to come and pick you up?"

"I'll drive. I'm on my way." Delta was nowhere in sight when Jo emerged from her office. She quickly scribbled a note, telling her she had an errand to run and would be back in a couple hours.

Jo dashed out the door with purse and keys in hand and let out a sigh of relief when the farm was in the rearview mirror. She would handle explaining to the others why she'd changed her mind about Laverne later.

Pastor Murphy was waiting in the front parking lot when Jo pulled around. "You got here fast."

"I decided it was best to make a quick escape before Delta found out. She's dead set against Laverne." Jo waited for him to buckle up before circling the drive and pulling onto the road.

"It's the kitchen thing," the pastor guessed.

"Among others. Raylene's comment about knowing Laverne the other night didn't help." Jo was backed into a corner with little choice other than seriously considering the woman.

She needed a body in the bed before Monday's inspection. If not, the state could shut her down. The lesser of the two evils was to bring Laverne on board. "Does Laverne know we're on our way?"

"No. Our visit will be a surprise. We're taking a chance that she'll refuse to see us," the pastor pointed out. "Although I doubt she'll do that."

The prison's parking lot was full, and Jo had to drive around twice before she found an empty spot. She shut the SUV off and reached for her purse. "Please, God, help me with this decision."

Once inside, Jo let Pastor Murphy do the talking. After clearing security, the doors unlocked, and they stepped into the visitor area. There was a brief wait before they were summoned to a private corner room.

The guard promised Laverne would be out shortly. They waited for five minutes. Then ten. Jo glanced at her watch. "Maybe she refused to see us."

"Let me see if I can find out what's going on." As the pastor reached for the desk phone, the door adjacent to where they were seated swung open.

Chapter 9

An armed guard escorted Laverne inside the room. She was dressed in drab prison garb, her face void of emotion. If she was surprised to see the pastor or Jo, she didn't show it.

"Visiting hours end in fifteen minutes." The guard stepped out of the room and closed the door behind him.

Laverne cautiously approached the table. "Hello."

Pastor Murphy peered at her over the rim of his glasses. "Hello, Laverne. How are you doing today?"

"I thought you were going to be here in the morning to pick me up."

"There's been a slight change in plans."

"You don't want me either?" Laverne asked bluntly.

"It's not that." Pastor Murphy cleared his throat. "Ms. Pepperdine is reconsidering taking you in. She wanted to chat with you before making a final decision."

Laverne pulled out a chair and plopped down. "Funny you should show up here because I've been thinking too. I'm not sure your place would be right for me."

Jo's jaw dropped. "What is that supposed to mean?"

"I heard you run your farm like a prison camp. Work, work, work. No outside visitors. No free time. The residents' salaries are pennies compared to what you keep for yourself."

Jo stared at her in disbelief. "The residents who live at the farm are quite happy," she snapped. "If not, they are certainly free to contact their probation officer and ask to be moved."

"Or run away," Laverne said.

"If you're alluding to one of my former residents, she made a foolish decision, and now she's paying for it."

Laverne nonchalantly leaned back and began inspecting her fingernails. "Just saying."

Jo angrily shoved the chair back and stood. "I'm wasting my time."

Pastor Murphy sprang to his feet and placed a light hand on Jo's arm. "I don't think Laverne meant anything by that. She has no idea how you run the farm."

"Nope," Laverne agreed. "I'm not saying I believe it. I'm repeating what I heard, and it's making me think maybe it isn't for me."

"I think you're wrong. You're making a huge mistake," the pastor warned.

"You have nowhere else to go," Jo pointed out.

"I got a friend who lives over in Pine Creek. I might head over there."

"Not while you're on probation," Pastor Murphy said. "You must move to an approved facility."

"Says who?"

"Have you talked to your probation officer?" Jo shook her head.

"I left him a message and am waiting to hear back."

"I give up." Jo threw her hands in the air and turned to go.

Pastor Murphy swung around, giving Laverne his full attention. "You blew your best shot at starting over. I'm not taking you in, either. Not after this outrageous display of ingratitude."

Laverne stared at them both for a long moment. The look of defiance vanished in an instant, and her face crumpled. "I've been dumped on my whole life.

I knew you didn't care about me. None of you care," her voice cracked. "That's what I figured."

Jo stormed across the room and reached for the door handle.

"I'm sorry, Ms. Pepperdine," Laverne said in a small voice. "I didn't mean what I said."

"Apology accepted." Jo yanked the door open.

"Please?"

Jo stopped in her tracks, her back to the woman as she began counting to ten.

"I'm just an angry, bitter old woman and an idiot to boot. I prayed to God he would find somewhere for me to go," she whispered.

Pastor Murphy watched as a silent war waged inside Jo.

She let go of the door handle and did an about-face. "Give me one good reason I should take you in."

"Because I'll be a model resident. I'll do whatever you ask. I'm a good cook. In fact, I worked in the prison kitchen."

"We already have one, Delta Childress."

"I heard about her. She used to be the prison cook," Laverne said. "She's kinda bossy."

"Which means you two will clash, and I don't need that sort of headache," Jo said.

Laverne ignored the comment. "I'm also a whiz at sewing and knitting. I've knitted baby caps for preemies at the hospital. I'm also computer savvy."

"Which could be a good thing or bad," Jo muttered under her breath. "You have some valuable job skills which will serve you well going forward."

"Perfect. I'll see you in the morning." Laverne stood.

"Hold up." Jo lifted a hand. "I haven't made a decision yet, and after your display of brat-itude just now, I'm leaning toward taking a pass."

"But you drove all the way over here, making a special trip. If you weren't seriously considering offering me a spot, why did you bother?"

"I'm beginning to wonder," Jo sighed.

"Let's start over. I'm willing to negotiate to reach an agreement."

"The reason I wanted to come here was to discuss the farm's rules and your list of demands."

"Requirements," Laverne primly corrected.

"All of the residents are given specific times and a schedule for television and the internet, which is in the evening after dinner and the businesses have closed for the day."

"But…"

Jo cut her off. "Secondly, if you need fragrance-free soaps and detergents, we can work on that.

Thirdly, there are already quiet hours in place for residents. If it's past your bedtime and others are still up, then go to your room."

Pastor Murphy chuckled under his breath.

Jo continued. "The farm's produce shouldn't be a problem. All of our fruits and vegetables are grown in our gardens."

"Great," Laverne said. "It appears I may have had the wrong impression about your place, after all."

"Number five on your list is going to be a problem," Jo said. "The kitchen is Delta's domain. The only way you'll be allowed to work in there is with her permission."

Laverne grunted. "I'm my most creative in the kitchen."

"Then, you can use the kitchenette in the residents' common area."

"Does it have all of the modern conveniences...a toaster oven, air fryer, a juicer? I can't live without a juicer. It would be torture to have all of those fresh fruits and vegetables at my fingertips and not have a juicer."

"I'll see what I can do," Jo bargained.

"Then I guess we hammered out the details," Laverne said. "To recap, I'll get my fragrance-free, hypoallergenic personal hygiene products, I'll have access to television and the internet, as well as a kitchen for creativity. Quiet time can be in my room."

"That about covers it," Jo said. She briefly explained how the work schedules were posted Sunday for the Monday workweek, she would be assigned to the workshop with Nash, the gardens with Gary, the bakeshop or mercantile and that she rotated with a different job each day.

"You'll be paid each Friday via direct deposit into a checking account we'll set up. You'll have access to your money, to be used on approved items."

"Approved items?" Laverne sputtered. "I can't buy what I want?"

"Within reason, as long as it doesn't involve contraband items such as cell phones, cigarettes or alcohol."

"No cell phone? What if I need to call someone?"

"You can use the house phone."

"Whew." Laverne blew air through thinned lips. "You're one tough cookie."

"Then find somewhere else to hang your hat."

"I... No, I mean, I'm sure you have good reasons for your rules."

"Precisely."

"Do you have them in writing, so I can take a look at them?"

"I do," Pastor Murphy removed a single sheet of paper from the briefcase he'd brought with him and slid it across the table.

Laverne scanned the sheet. "Yeah. This is what you said."

Jo reached into her purse, pulled out an ink pen and handed it to Laverne. "Sign and date the sheet, acknowledging you've read and agreed to my rules."

"Seriously?"

"I want to make sure you understand and intend to abide by them."

"Oh, brother." Laverne pressed her palm to her forehead. "What am I getting myself into?"

Pastor Murphy frowned. "You're treading on thin ice again, Laverne."

"Whatever." Laverne began to hum under her breath. She signed the paper with a flourish and then slid it back across the table.

Jo picked it up and studied the signature. "Laverne Belk. I thought your name was Laverne Huntsman."

"Belk is my maiden name."

"I'm not playing games," Jo gritted out. "Sign using your legal name."

"Picky, picky, picky," Laverne muttered under her breath and began to write. She placed the pen on top and slid both back toward her for a second time. "Signed, sealed, delivered, I'm yours."

"I may live to regret this moment." Jo carefully folded the paper in thirds and tucked it, along with the pen, into her purse.

"I'll see you in the morning?" Laverne asked. "I'm being released at nine."

"I'll be here to pick you up," the pastor said. "We'll drive from here to the farm where Jo and the other residents will be waiting for your arrival."

"Cool beans. Can't wait to meet the new gang." Laverne offered them a toothy smile. "Sorry for getting off on the wrong foot, Ms. P. I just have a personal policy to make sure no one gets the impression they can walk all over Laverne B. Huntsman."

"We'll see you tomorrow morning, Laverne." The pastor led the way out of the visiting room and closed the door behind them. "That went surprisingly well."

"Really?" Jo arched a brow. "I was ready to walk two minutes into the meeting."

"But Laverne apologized. She's a little rough around the edges."

"And all the way in between." Jo pressed the tips of her fingers to her temples. "I'm beginning to wonder what I'm getting myself into. Now, I'll have to go home and let everyone know Laverne is arriving in the morning."

Kelli, Michelle, Leah, as well as Gary and Nash had no preconceived opinions about Laverne. Raylene and Delta, on the other hand, had an inkling of what they were getting into, but even then, Jo had a sneaking suspicion it was just the tip of the iceberg.

Unless Laverne changed her tune, Jo was certain they were in for a few weeks' worth of rough rides and a period of adjustment. Even more so than some of the past residents.

"Would you like me to be there for the meeting, to kind of smooth things over?" the pastor asked.

"I appreciate the offer, but I think I'll be all right. Except for Delta. She's my biggest concern."

"I can see those two butting heads," Pastor Murphy said.

"That may be an understatement." Jo dropped the pastor off where she'd picked him up, in front of the church and then headed home. During the drive, Jo mentally rehearsed what she would say. Presentation was everything, and if she put a positive spin on it, perhaps she would set the tone, and things would run smoothly.

"Who am I kidding?" Jo asked herself. "This is going to be a train wreck."

Her stomach was in knots by the time she reached the farm. It was almost dinnertime, and she decided to wait until they were all seated at the table to make the big announcement.

Thankfully, Delta was distracted in the kitchen and only briefly asked Jo where she'd been, to which she gave a vague answer.

It was spaghetti and meatball night, with a tossed salad and garlic bread. Jo pitched in to set the table as the residents, along with Gary and Nash, began making their way to the dining room.

Delta was the last to be seated, and Nash waited until she joined them to pray a blessing over the food.

After he finished, Jo slowly stood. "Before we eat, I have an important announcement to make."

Chapter 10

"I've agreed to allow Laverne Huntsman to move to the farm." Jo braced herself for the reaction, but there was none.

Everyone at the table stared at her in disbelief. It was so quiet, Jo could've heard a pin drop.

Finally, Raylene spoke. "Laverne Huntsman," she repeated.

"Yes. Pastor Murphy will be picking her up and bringing her here tomorrow morning after she's released from prison."

"You're kidding," Delta said. "I thought you were dead set against her."

"I had a change of heart after praying about it. Besides, I...we need her as much as she needs us." Jo briefly explained the state was conducting its annual inspection the following Monday. "We need a seventy-five percent occupancy rate to pass the state's requirements. If we don't, they could pull my license and shut us down."

"And we would have to leave," Kelli said.

"Correct. I'm between a rock and a hard place. There are no other releases in the foreseeable future. It was either bring Laverne on board or risk being shut down."

"Well, you know where I stand." Delta drummed her fingers on the table. "We're gonna have to make lemonade out of a batch of lemons."

"I spoke with Laverne at length earlier. She understands and has agreed to abide by the farm's rules."

Jo continued. "We reached a compromise on her list of demands. She has allergies, so I told her I would order special personal hygiene products to get her started. As far as quiet time, I told her if she needs quiet time, she could retreat to her room. The organic fruits and vegetables won't be a problem since all of our produce is organic."

"What about unlimited access to my kitchen?" Delta interrupted.

"Your kitchen is off-limits unless you want her to help you. Otherwise, she can explore her kitchen creativity in the common area kitchenette." Jo clasped her hands as she gazed around the table. "I need everyone's cooperation. Laverne may go through a...period of adjustment. I'm counting on all of you. In the meantime, we still have one open spot, and Pastor Murphy is working to help me fill it just in case..."

"In case Laverne doesn't work out," Leah finished.

"Correct. I can't over-emphasize how important it is that Laverne is welcomed with open arms and an open mind. I'm hopeful we'll all be pleasantly surprised."

"We'll do whatever it takes," Raylene promised. "At least I will."

Me too," Kelli nodded.

The other women agreed.

"You know I'm on your side, Jo," Gary said. "We'll do what we have to to make it work."

"Absolutely," Nash chimed in. "It isn't as if we haven't faced our share of challenges before. This is just one more."

"Thank you," Jo clasped her hands and turned to Delta. "Well? Are you onboard?"

"I most certainly am," Delta said. "We're in this together. Besides, one itty bitty irritating woman ain't about to stop us now."

Jo grinned. "I couldn't agree more. I'll be working on the engagement party I'm hosting here at the farm Sunday afternoon. Delta's given me some ideas. I figured I could get some input from everyone else as far as who should be invited."

Gary gave Jo a few names. The women threw out a few "regulars" they thought should be invited. After dinner, Jo attempted to help Delta and the women clean up, but they shooed her out of the kitchen.

"Go work on that party," Delta urged. "It's time to celebrate."

Despite the nagging worry about her new resident, Jo's excitement over the upcoming nuptials and celebration took over. After all, it wasn't every day that two of Jo's best friends decided to tie the knot.

The marriage would be a new beginning for the couple. Gary's wife, Teresa, had died of cancer, leaving him lonely and alone until Jo purchased the old McDougall place and transformed it into a home for the former convicts.

Jo still remembered the day he pulled up in his old truck and offered to help. She'd immediately taken a liking to Gary, and after she learned he was a widower, she took him under her wing, treating him like family – family she didn't have.

She sorted through several online websites for invitations and found one with a tractor and wagon, with the headline, "They're getting hitched!"

Jo called Gary and Delta into her office for a quick consultation, and they both wholeheartedly agreed the farm theme was perfect. She downloaded the invitation and then added the emails and names of everyone she planned to invite. She uploaded a picture of the couple she'd taken on the porch when they first started dating, and after making sure that everything looked perfect, she sent them out.

She had just finished when she heard a light tap on the door. It was Nash. "Am I interrupting?"

"Of course not. I sent out the invitations for the engagement party. It's this coming Sunday at three." Jo showed him a copy. "I had no idea we knew so many people."

Nash casually leaned against the window seat and crossed his arms. "And growing by the day. I'm here to offer you my support regarding your decision to bring Laverne on board."

"Thanks, Nash. I prayed about it. Believe me when I tell you the last thing I want is to bring a troublesome woman to the farm. My back is against the wall. I have no choice. It was either Laverne or no one, and I can't risk losing my license." Jo rubbed the back of her neck. "We'll have to take it one day at a time."

Nash changed the subject. "How is Sherry? I heard you ran over there first thing this morning to check on her after she chatted with Raylene last night."

Jo shared her concerns, how Sherry thought someone was lurking out back as well as out front. "Someone damaged her mailbox."

"Her mailbox?"

"They tried to pry it open."

"That could be kids messing around," Nash said.

"I hope you're right. I hope it was just a bunch of kids." Jo remembered Claire's comment and told him that a local had been complaining about the "riff-raff."

"I'm sure there are one or two. You can't control the attitudes of the locals. Sherry will have to prove herself." Nash turned to go. "I need to run over to Dave Kilwin's farm to borrow a finishing tool. I shouldn't be gone long."

Jo followed him to the office door, where he gave her a quick kiss before sauntering down the hallway. After he left, Jo began assembling Laverne's folder and placed the list of house rules the woman had signed inside.

Pastor Murphy had forwarded Laverne's records and other information he'd collected during his visits. It included a copy of the penitentiary's emergency contact sheet Laverne had filled out when she arrived there. The lines were blank. At the very bottom in neatly printed words were, "No family. No friends. No one to contact."

Jo swallowed the lump in her throat. She knew exactly how Laverne felt; she'd felt the same way after her father's death and her mother's incarceration, followed by her mother's sudden death. Other than a distant uncle who lived in Texas, she had no family until Miles had shown up on her doorstep.

Jo's adopted family was her family...the residents, Delta, Gary and Nash, not to mention the many friends she'd made since moving to Divine. This was her home. They were her family.

She stared at the blank lines, Pastor Murphy's words echoing in her head. Laverne was determined to keep a wall between herself and others so she wouldn't get hurt.

She thought about the desperation in the woman's voice near the end of their visit. The look in her eyes. The false bravado.

An overwhelming sense of calm filled Jo. It was going to be all right. God had a hand in this, and it was up to him to help her sort through her emotional issues.

Delta appeared in the doorway. "Gary and I are heading over to his place so I can have a look around."

"A pre-marital inspection," Jo joked.

"Something like that." Delta had confided in Jo that Gary admitted his house needed some updating, a woman's touch after years of it being just him, and she was thrilled at the thought of having a home of her own, not one shared with her niece – or Jo.

"I'm happy for you, Delta. You'll have your very own home."

"Thanks. I can't wait, not that I don't love living here."

"I know you do, but there's nothing like a place of your own."

Shortly after Delta departed, Jo trailed behind, heading to the front porch for some fresh air and a few quiet moments. Duke followed her out. She waited for the pup to settle onto the swing before joining him.

Off in the distance, a bolt of lightning lit the night sky. A low rumble of thunder followed.

It was the peak of tornado season and so far Divine, which was on the outskirts of "Tornado Alley," had been blessed to have missed the destructive forces of the past few weeks.

The wind picked up, swirling the leaves and causing them to dance along the edge of the sidewalk until being caught up in the sunflowers and wildflowers Delta had recently planted.

Duke buried his head and let out a whimper at the next rumble of thunder.

"I think a storm is brewing, Duke." She'd just gotten up when she spied headlights bouncing off the side of the barn. It was Nash, returning in his truck. He parked off to the side, next to the workshop. Jo flicked the porch lights.

Nash changed direction and strode across the gravel drive. "Storm's coming."

"Duke and I were just contemplating running for cover."

Nash gently moved Duke to the side, and he and Jo sat down. "After I stopped by Dave's place, I ran into town to fill up on gas. I noticed the lights on at your brother's theater, so I swung by there. Won't be long and he'll have the place up and running."

"Yes. He's doing a great job."

"He was there with some other guy." Nash patted Duke's head.

"With brownish-gray hair and balding on top?"

"Yes."

"That's Chet Cleaper, the guy I asked you about. He's still helping Miles?"

"It would appear so." Nash gave a quick look around. "Where's Delta?"

"She and Gary went over to his place. She's looking forward to sprucing it up and making it her own."

"Can't say as I blame her. Have you ever been inside Gary's house?"

"Once, when he was in the hospital, but I don't remember much about it."

"It's a time capsule from the early seventies. Orange and yellow and red all over."

A smattering of rain pelted the ground. There was a flash of lightning. Duke scrambled off the swing and ran to the front door. The couple dashed inside to wait out the storm. After it passed, they returned to the porch.

Jo closed her eyes and breathed deeply. "There's nothing like a summer shower to clear the air."

The couple made small talk about the engagement party, the new resident and the planting season. Jo stifled a yawn. "I'm sorry. It's been a long day. I wonder how much longer Delta will be."

She no more than got the words out of her mouth when she heard the roar of an engine off in the distance. Gary's truck careened into the driveway, coming to an abrupt halt.

The passenger door flew open. Delta sprang from the vehicle, turning back once to face the driver. "Then maybe it's time for us to rethink this whole getting wed before we're dead plan."

Delta slammed the door shut and marched up the porch steps, never even looking in Jo and Nash's direction as she stormed into the house.

Chapter 11

"Looks like Delta and Nash are having a lover's spat," Nash guessed.

"I think you're right." Jo slid Duke to the side and made her way down the steps. She and Nash met Gary, who had exited his truck, near the driver's side door. "What happened?"

"I dunno. One minute, Delta's talking about hanging some new curtains. Next thing I know, she's telling me she wants to go home."

"Something must have happened," Jo insisted.

Gary scratched his head. "It all started when I told her I saw nothing wrong with the curtains Teresa sewed. If you ask me, roosters are fitting drapery for farmhouse windows."

"So, Delta wanted to put up new curtains, and you didn't want her to."

"No sense in getting rid of perfectly good curtains." Gary grabbed hold of his suspenders. "They've been hanging there pretty as a picture for decades now. In fact, Teresa loved those curtains."

"Something tells me there might be more."

"Well, then she started talking about bringing some new pots and pans over, stuff she's had packed away for some time now."

"You don't want Delta's pots and pans," Nash guessed.

"It's not that I don't want them, but the cast iron set I got Teresa on our thirtieth wedding anniversary has stood the test of time."

"Gary, Gary..." Jo slowly shook her head. "Delta's never been married, never had a home to call her own. Pots and pans and curtains that belong to her mean a lot."

"You mean she's upset about curtains and pots and pans?" Gary's eyes grew wide.

"She wants to make the house *her* home, not Teresa's, not that she has anything against your wife."

"It's a woman thing, I think," Nash chimed in.

"It's a woman thing," Jo echoed.

"So, you're telling me that I should let her do what she wants?"

"Within reason, if you want to marry Delta and maintain marital harmony."

"Oh, I most certainly do." Gary nodded enthusiastically. "I had no idea she felt that way."

Nash placed a hand on Gary's back and propelled him forward. "Go on in there and patch things up. Tell her she can change all the curtains and bring in as many pots and pans as she likes."

"Heck, she can even swap out my old garden tractor if she wants." Gary hurried up the steps and disappeared inside.

"Crisis averted," Jo joked.

"Us guys don't always understand the girlie stuff," Nash tapped the side of his forehead. "Sometimes, it takes a rap upside the head to get the point across."

Thankfully, there were no loud crashes, yelling or harsh words coming from the house. A sheepish Gary and calm Delta joined them a short time later, holding hands.

"We got everything all ironed out," Gary said.

"It was a minor misunderstanding," Delta chimed in.

"It happens to the best of us," Jo yawned loudly. "Excuse me. I think it's way past my bedtime."

Nash gave Jo's hand a gentle squeeze and a light kiss. "I'll see you in the morning."

Jo returned inside, and Delta wasn't far behind. "I'm sorry for causing a scene. I was just upset."

"Gary didn't understand how important it is for a woman to feel her home is her own, that she's not stepping into the shadow of another woman."

"Right. He said that. He's letting me change whatever I want. His kids will want to keep some of their mother's belongings, and it's not like I'm trying to erase her, just find my own place."

"There's absolutely nothing wrong with that."

"Thanks for helping iron things out." Delta shifted her feet. "I gotta get a grip on my hot head and not blab whatever is on my mind."

"It makes you, you. I wouldn't worry about it. The good news is, we all know exactly where we stand." Jo gave her friend a quick hug and began making her rounds, checking the doors to make sure she'd locked up before she and Duke headed upstairs.

Despite the busyness and stress of the day, Jo slept soundly and woke early.

Since Delta wasn't up yet, she tiptoed around the kitchen, starting a pot of coffee. Once it finished brewing, she filled a cup, and she and Duke headed to the front porch. It had rained during the night, leaving traces of moisture on the grass, the flowerbeds and bushes lining the porch railing.

She sipped her coffee, savoring the quiet of the morning. Today was the big day...Laverne's arrival. She prayed the transition would go smoothly, and the new resident would put in a hundred percent effort in adjusting to life on the farm.

Jo downed the last of her coffee and then ran next door to inspect Tara's old unit, the unit Laverne would be occupying. She checked to make sure there were clean sheets, and the dresser drawers and closets were empty. She finished with a quick inspection of the common area and the medicine cabinet that would be assigned to her.

Curtis, the farm's new fur family member, joined Jo during her inspection.

She knelt down to scratch her ears as the cat wound her way around her ankles. "Are you ready for someone new to spoil you?" She filled Curtis' food and water bowls and headed to the door, bumping into Leah, who was on her way in.

"Good morning, Jo."

"Good morning, Leah. I was inspecting the bathrooms and common area, getting ready for Laverne's arrival this morning. You're up bright and early."

"Today is my gardens day." Leah loved working in the gardens with Gary and hoped to one day own a farm of her own.

Her plans included a self-sufficient compound that featured organic produce and implemented green practices. She once told Jo that she wanted to leave a small footprint, living as close to "off the grid" as possible.

"How are the gardens growing?" Jo teased.

"Great." Leah's eyes lit. "We've been experimenting with some new compost materials. Would you like to check it out?"

"Of course." Jo was thrilled with Leah's enthusiasm and made a point of supporting each of her residents' interests, hoping that someday they would turn into something more. "I would love to see what you two have come up with."

She followed Leah out and pulled the door shut. "I think you and Gary should enter this year's fall pumpkin contest."

"That would be fun. We're putting in a large pumpkin patch. I love the fall harvest." Leah chattered on about the gardens and how Gary was teaching her to drive the tractor. "I was thinking..."

"Thinking what?" Jo prompted.

"Never mind."

"No," Jo said. "I want to hear your thoughts. They're important."

"Well, we were talking about maybe adding a chicken coop and some chickens for eggs." Leah hurried on. "We could put them near the back, so you won't have to listen to the rooster crowing early in the morning."

"I like the idea."

"You do?"

"Sure." Jo shrugged. "We could sell farm fresh eggs."

"Thanks, Jo. You won't be sorry. I already did some research. We can charge at least three dollars for a dozen eggs since they'll be cage-free."

They reached the larger of the two gardens and a compost bin near the sunflower patch.

"This is it." Leah opened the bin's door, and the overpowering aroma of sulfur filled the air.

Jo gasped and clamped a hand across her mouth. "Oh, my gosh."

"It's pretty strong right now."

"It smells like rotten eggs."

Leah calmly propped the door open. "The smell takes a little getting used to. Gary and I plan to aerate it this morning, but since it rained last night, I think the compost might be too wet." She reached inside and grabbed a handful of slimy green material.

Jo watched it drip from her fingers and could feel her stomach start to churn. She stumbled back. "I can't..."

"It is kind of gross." Leah tossed the pile of green slop back on top.

Jo nodded, her eyes watering. "Yes. Yes, it is."

"After aerating, we'll add more dry material, which should take care of the smell." While Leah explained the benefits of composting and how it was mixed, Jo tried to focus on what she was saying, and not what her stomach was telling her.

Leah finished explaining the process. She shut the bin's door and secured the latch.

"I learned something new, Leah," Jo said. "Thank you for teaching me about composting."

The women stopped by the garden shed, where Leah washed her hands in the small sink. They headed to the house and found Delta buzzing around the kitchen. The tantalizing aroma of frying bacon was a welcome relief from the horrible stench of the compost bin.

Breakfast was a lively affair, with the main topic of conversation being the upcoming engagement party. Jo mentioned the chickens and farm fresh eggs to which the group unanimously agreed it was a great idea.

It was nearly nine, and the breakfast table had been cleared when Pastor Murphy texted Jo to let her know he was on his way to pick up Laverne and that they would be arriving right on time.

Jo wandered through the house, straightening lamps, fluffing throw pillows and stopping by the front window every few minutes to check for cars.

Delta stopped her on her third time around the living room. "You look like you're waiting for the executioner," she teased.

"I am nervous," Jo said.

"We could pray about it," Kelli suggested.

"Maybe we should."

The women gathered in a circle and joined hands.

"Dear Lord," Delta prayed. "Laverne is on her way. Please be with us today, as we all become acquainted. I ask that you guide us and continue to bring peace and harmony to all who reside here."

"And that Laverne won't drive us all crazy," Jo added.

"Amen," Delta heartily agreed.

"We got this," Raylene said.

"No doubt," Kelli added.

Jo's cell phone chimed again. "It's Pastor Murphy. He just pulled into the drive. It's time to greet our new resident."

Chapter 12

The residents waited in the living room while Jo stepped onto the porch to greet Pastor Murphy and Laverne. The pastor retrieved a bag from the trunk and motioned to Laverne to join Jo, who was waiting for them at the top of the steps.

"Good morning," Jo offered them a warm smile. "You're right on time."

"Hello." Laverne shaded her eyes and studied her surroundings. "This isn't what I pictured at all."

"What did you picture?"

"I dunno. A rundown, dumpy, dilapidated farm with a bunch of chickens running around."

"We don't have any farm animals, except for Duke and a cat named Curtis." Jo patted the pup's head. "At least not yet."

"Dogs don't usually like me." Laverne pressed her arms to her sides as Duke trotted over to investigate the new arrival. He gave the woman a tentative sniff and then greeted the pastor.

"Duke gave you his sniff of approval," Jo joked.

"That's a first." Laverne relaxed her stance.

"The pastor and I will show you to your private quarters, give you a tour and then introduce you to the other residents." Jo could see the living room curtains flutter as she led the pastor and Laverne to the housing units located behind the bakeshop and mercantile.

She unlocked the door to Laverne's unit and then stepped off to the side. "This is your private room."

"Thanks." Laverne squeezed past Jo. "Not bad." She placed her bag on the bed and then peeked inside the closet. "It's nice. A lot nicer than what I was staying in before."

Jo smiled. "I'm sure it is. Let me show you the common area." While they walked, Jo explained the common area was available to the residents twenty-four/seven. "There's a small kitchen which is available to all residents, although most of the meals are eaten in the main house." She rattled off the set breakfast and dinner hour.

Laverne interrupted. "Do I have to eat with everyone?"

"No. Of course not, although Delta is a wonderful cook and it would be a shame for you to miss out on her meals."

"Delta," Laverne repeated.

"Delta Childress. She runs the household and is our cook. She also bakes the goods we sell in the bakeshop. I think you mentioned hearing her name."

"You're right. I have. She worked as the prison's cook for years."

"Until she retired and joined me here at the farm."

"She's got a reputation."

Jo arched a brow. "At the prison?"

"Oh, yeah." Laverne nodded. "Like I said before, I worked in the kitchen and heard her name more than once. She ran a tight ship."

"She does here, as well, which is another reason you're not allowed free reign of the kitchen. It's Delta's domain. She sets the kitchen schedule."

"Thanks for the heads up. I can promise you I won't be messing with her."

Jo showed her the bathrooms, the shower stalls and then the medicine cabinet assigned to her. "I've ordered fragrance and dye-free laundry soap and personal hygiene products for you, which will be coming in today or tomorrow. After that, you'll be on your own to purchase the items."

"Thanks. I'm looking forward to switching from the chemical-laden junk the prison passed out as personal care products."

Curtis emerged from beneath the dining table and stalked across the room. Jo scooped him up and held him close. "This is Curtis. She's a stray someone dropped off at the farm. She adopted us a couple months ago."

"Curtis is a she?" Laverne asked.

"It's a long story, but yes, Curtis is a female. Curtis is allowed to wander around the farm but prefers to spend most of her time in here."

Laverne patted the cat's head, and she began to purr. "I think she likes me."

They finished touring the women's common area, with Jo showing her the computers, the cleaning schedule and then they circled around to the businesses.

Kelli was in the mercantile, getting ready to open for the day. She waited for them to join her. "Good morning."

"Laverne Huntsman, this is Kelli."

"Hello," Laverne offered her a cautious smile.

"Welcome to the farm."

"Thank you. I'm glad to be here, to be somewhere other than locked up."

They made their way next door to where Raylene was loading the bakeshop display case. Polite introductions were made, and then they wandered out of the building. "The rest of the residents are in the house."

They passed through the empty living room and dining room, making their way into the kitchen, where Leah and Michelle stood at the counter, placing muffins onto a tray.

Delta was nearby, loading the dishwasher.

Jo cleared her throat. "Everyone, I would like you to meet our newest resident, Laverne Huntsman."

The women stopped what they were doing and waited while Jo introduced each of them. She started with Leah and Michelle and ended with Delta, who gave the woman the once over. "Welcome to the best place on the planet."

"Thank you," Laverne replied. "I have to say I'm pleasantly surprised by how nice the facilities are after what I heard at the prison."

"By some former resident who messed up and ended up back behind bars," Delta said.

"That's true." Laverne eyed the mixing bowl on the counter. "What are you making?"

"Morning glory muffins."

"Those sound delicious, Delta." Pastor Murphy patted his stomach.

"I've got one with your name on it." Delta reached behind Leah and plucked a muffin from the tray. "Would you like one too?" she asked Laverne.

"I...if you don't mind. They do look tasty."

"I'll pour some coffee." Jo grabbed clean cups from the cabinet while Delta arranged the muffins on a plate.

"The bakeshop is getting ready to open. We need to get these next door." Leah and Michelle carried the trays of decadent goodies out while the others gathered around the kitchen table.

Laverne smacked her lips as she carefully peeled the paper liner off. She took a tentative bite and closed her eyes. "This is delicious. I haven't tasted a morning glory muffin in years."

"Thanks. It's my secret recipe," Delta beamed. "The muffins are best sellers in the bakeshop."

Jo breathed a sigh of relief. The introduction she'd been most concerned about was Laverne and Delta's. She caught Pastor Murphy's eye. He winked, and she knew he was thinking the same thing.

Laverne took a cautious sip of coffee and then another bite. "I will have to say I think it needs a touch more coconut and tart apple."

Delta's expression morphed from pleasant to combative in a matter of seconds. A storm was brewing, and Pastor Murphy must have realized it too. "I think they're perfect, Delta. Why, you could enter these in this fall's baking contest and win hands down." He polished off the last bite and reached for his napkin.

"Yes, they most definitely could," Jo quickly added.

Laverne seemed not to notice Delta's mood change as she rattled on about baking and how she'd like to enter a baking contest too. The exchange couldn't end quickly enough for Jo. As soon as Laverne finished the last bite, she shoved her chair back and abruptly stood. "We should let Delta get back to work."

The pastor hastily joined her. "Yes, and I need to get going. I have a meeting at the church."

"I need to tinkle," Laverne announced on their way out.

"There's a guest powder room around the corner. We'll be out on the porch." Jo waited until Laverne disappeared around the corner, and she and the pastor were alone before speaking. "That was a close call." She pretended to swipe her hand across her brow.

"No kidding. I was waiting for Delta to rip the muffin right out of Laverne's hand," Pastor Murphy joked. "You'll need to remind your new resident to tread lightly."

"Believe me, I will."

Laverne joined them, and they accompanied the pastor to his car. "I have a meeting with the warden early next week to go over the list of potential new residents. By then, you should all be settled."

"Yes. Hopefully, it will be an easy transition." Jo glanced at her new resident.

Pastor Murphy gave them both an encouraging smile as he climbed behind the wheel. "I'll touch base soon."

As he drove off, Jo addressed her new resident. "Our first order of business is to fill out some paperwork, and then I'll take you around to meet Nash, the handyman who lives here, and Gary, who handles the gardens and yards."

They stepped back inside, and Jo could hear Delta grumbling loudly over the clanging of pots and pans. There was a crash, followed by more loud noises.

"My office is this way." Jo led Laverne down the hall and made her way behind the desk. "Please. Have a seat."

Laverne perched on the edge of a nearby chair as she looked around. "This is a nice setup. I like all the antiques. It must have cost you a pretty penny to trick this place out."

"It was a labor of love." Jo unlocked a cabinet drawer, reached inside and removed Laverne's folder. She grabbed a set of keys and handed them to the woman. "These are your keys. One is to your unit. I suggest you keep it locked when you're not there."

"Because you think one of the other residents will start messing around?"

"No, they would have no reason to go into your unit. I run two businesses, which means there are people who aren't residents of the farm coming and going during all hours of the day. It's a safeguard to keep strangers out."

"Right. Right."

"The other key is for your medicine cabinet. As I mentioned earlier, your special soaps and detergents will arrive sometime today or tomorrow. If they show up today, I'll give them to you after dinner."

"Yeah, about that part..." Laverne shifted. "I'm not sure about this whole eating together and bonding thing. I'm more of a loner."

"Eating in the main dining room will help you get to know the other residents and staff and make your adjustment easier."

"I dunno."

Jo let it go. For whatever reason, the woman was dead set against eating her meals with the others. Somewhere down the line, Jo would figure out why. She had a sneaking suspicion it had nothing to do with the farm.

She reviewed the rules, the ones Laverne had signed off on the previous day. Jo briefly told her how the job rotation schedule worked and that her pay would be direct deposited in a checking account she would set up for her.

"You'll start your first job tomorrow morning after breakfast. I'm going to ask Kelli to train you in the bakeshop. The following day, you'll switch over to the mercantile, training with another resident. Since you're into organic foods, you'll be happy to know you'll work with Gary in the gardens, Nash in the workshop and perhaps even Delta in the kitchen."

Laverne perked up. "Now that's something I'm looking forward to. The kitchen."

"If Delta asks for your help," Jo warned.

"Why wouldn't she? I have plenty of experience in the prison kitchen, just like her. Why, I think we'll be like two peas in a pod."

"We'll see." Jo didn't want to squash Laverne's excitement about working with Delta. Judging by Delta's reaction to Laverne's criticism, she could already envision the eventual fireworks.

Jo's cell phone chimed. She picked it up and glanced at the screen. She didn't recognize the number and hit dismiss. Seconds later, she received a text message:

"Hey, Jo. It's Wayne Malton. Please give me a call as soon as you get this message."

"Excuse me for a minute." Jo scrolled the screen and dialed Wayne's number. He answered on the first ring. "Hey, Jo. Thanks for getting back with me so fast."

"You're welcome. I'm sorry I didn't recognize your number. What's up?"

"Remember how I said I was going to adjust my surveillance cameras to keep an eye on the apartments?" Wayne didn't wait for Jo to reply. "Well, I did. I'm at the hardware store and just finished reviewing the recordings this morning. I think there's something you should see."

Chapter 13

Jo's heart skipped a beat. "I'm wrapping up a meeting and will be on my way in a few minutes." She thanked Wayne before ending the call. "I'm sorry, but I have an urgent matter to attend to. Why don't you head to your unit, settle in and unpack?"

"Sure." Laverne shrugged. "Now, as far as the kitchen goes..."

"Delta's kitchen is strictly off-limits, but feel free to familiarize yourself with the common area kitchenette." Jo accompanied her new resident as far as the front steps. "I shouldn't be long. When I return, I'll introduce you to Nash and Gary. By then, I'm sure you'll have some questions."

Laverne thanked Jo before sauntering off, whistling under her breath as she strolled across the lawn.

Jo darted back inside. She stopped by her office to grab the truck keys and then made a beeline for the kitchen.

Delta stood in front of the fridge, notepad in hand. "Are you heading out?"

"I'm on my way to the hardware store. Wayne called and said he caught something on the surveillance cameras last night."

"Caught something on camera?"

"I stopped by there to chat with him yesterday and told him Sherry thought someone was lurking across the street. Wayne decided to set up one of his cameras to keep an eye on the apartments. He thinks he has something."

Delta slammed the door shut. "Mind if I tag along?"

"The more, the merrier." Jo told her she'd meet her by the truck and then stopped by the workshop. "Hey, Nash." Jo jangled the truck keys. "Delta and I are heading into town."

"I thought you were bringing the new resident around."

"When I get back. Wayne caught something on the cameras last night he thinks I should see."

"You mean at Sherry's place?" Nash set the sander on the table and lifted his goggles.

Jo nodded. "Delta is going with me. Laverne is in her unit, unpacking."

"I'll keep an eye out in case she needs something."

"Thanks. We shouldn't be long."

Delta was already in the truck waiting for Jo. "What did you do with high maintenance?"

"High maintenance?"

"Laverne."

"Now, Delta," Jo chided. "She's in her unit, settling in. We went over the farm rules and the paper she signed yesterday. You'll be happy to know that I stressed to her that your kitchen was off-limits unless she got a personal invite."

"Thanks." Delta buckled her seatbelt. "Something tells me it probably went in one ear and out the other."

"You could be right." Jo consulted the rearview mirror before backing onto the driveway. "She strikes me as somewhat set in her ways."

"What was she in for?"

As a rule, Jo did not share the details of the residents' reasons for incarceration without their permission. In fact, she encouraged them to share their story with the others the first night they arrived. Something told her Laverne had no plans to be forthright about her conviction.

This was why Jo required the residents to sign a form, stating they gave permission for her to discuss their history with staff at the farm, as well as local authorities and clergy, meaning Pastor Murphy.

"Forgery and employee theft."

"Forgery."

"Laverne was a live-in caretaker for a wealthy elderly woman in Kansas City. The woman died, and when the heirs, her children, started digging around, they discovered Laverne had helped herself to a substantial sum of the woman's money, including from bank accounts. She also forged her signature to obtain credit cards."

Delta let out a low whistle. "No kidding. Well, you had better watch your back. If she finds out how much money you have, you might become her next target."

Jo tightened her grip on the steering wheel. The thought had already crossed her mind. "The only way she'll find out is if someone tells her."

"It ain't gonna come from these lips." Delta made a zipping motion.

When they arrived in town, Jo found an empty parking spot in front of the hardware store. She waited for Delta on the sidewalk, and the two made their way inside, where they found Wayne stocking shelves near the front window. "That was fast."

"It sounded important, so I dropped everything."

Wayne led them to a small office in the back. He reached under the counter and removed a laptop. "I've watched the recording a couple times now. At first, it seemed like nothing, but after studying it a second time, I noticed something."

He shifted the laptop, turning it so the women could see. The screen was dark, with only a dim light beaming up. "The lights in the corner are from Sherry's apartment. The one on the opposite end belongs to my other tenant, Todd."

"I met him yesterday. He's an odd duck."

"He's quiet, kind of a loner. He came in to buy some batteries, rope and twist ties."

Jo's head shot up. "Rope and twist ties?"

"I thought the same thing. When I questioned him about it, he told me he was shoring up a large house plant that had been damaged during his move."

"Hmm." Jo squinted her eyes and studied a brown splotch in the lower corner of the monitor. "What's that?"

"You'll see in a minute." Wayne pressed the play button, and the lights flickered. The brown blob moved to the right. It stopped and then turned.

She caught a glimpse of a side profile. "Someone is standing near the deli, watching this place."

"It appears that way."

The video continued with the solitary figure watching the building. A minute passed. The person inched across the screen and disappeared from sight.

"I'll play it again." Wayne replayed the video. "I'm not sure if you noticed the time stamp, but this was recorded around eleven-thirty last night."

"Which means Sherry and her neighbor, Todd, the one who purchased the rope and twist ties, were both still awake."

"It would appear so, at least their lights were on."

"I need a visual." Jo, along with Wayne and Delta, returned to the front picture window overlooking the sidewalk and Main Street. "Where was the person standing?"

Wayne stepped in next to Jo and pointed. "Right about there."

"Which would give him or her an unobstructed view of the upstairs units."

"As well as the hardware store," Wayne added.

"Did you tell Sherry what you saw?" Jo asked.

"I haven't. I didn't want to freak her out. I figured I would talk to you first."

"She needs to know," Delta said.

"Yes, she does." Wayne told the women he'd reinforced the tenants' mailboxes and double-checked the upstairs exterior door lock. "It's a solid deadbolt. Someone would have to bust the door down to get in."

Jo thought about Sherry's insistence that someone was lurking outside, the damage to her mailbox, and now this – confirmation someone was watching the building.

"Maybe we should report it to the authorities," Delta craned her neck, peering across the street.

"And tell them what?" Jo asked. "That someone is watching the building? Other than damaging Sherry's mailbox, no crime has occurred." She thanked Wayne, who promised to continue surveilling the area at night, and the women wandered out onto the sidewalk.

"Sherry is working a double shift," Jo glanced at her watch. "I don't want to upset her and have her worrying about this all day. I would rather wait until later to mention it to her."

"What do you think about asking Sherry to stay at the farm?"

Jo trudged back to the truck, and the women climbed in. "Isn't that defeating the whole purpose of her going out on her own? Besides, maybe these incidents aren't related, and it's nothing."

"Or maybe it's something."

"I have an idea." Jo snapped her fingers. "What if we ask one of the other residents to stay with her for a couple days to make sure there's nothing going on?"

"Raylene," Delta and Jo said in unison.

"She would be the best choice, not to mention she and Sherry are close."

"Right," Delta nodded. "And there's safety in numbers."

"Raylene is sharp. She'll pick up on anything suspicious." The thought of Raylene staying with Sherry made Jo feel better. Raylene had the background and experience to handle almost any situation that might come along.

When they returned home, they found the parking lot nearly full, so Jo squeezed into a parking spot between two minivans. "It looks like business is booming."

"Word must've spread that I baked a batch of morning glory muffins," Delta joked.

"And they were delicious. Hopefully, they're almost already sold out. We need sales to start picking up." Jo waited for Delta to grab the bag of birdseed she had left by the back door before following her into the house.

She didn't realize her friend had abruptly stopped and plowed into her, nearly bowling them both over.

Delta quickly recovered and dropped the birdseed on the kitchen floor. "What in the world?"

Chapter 14

The upper half of Laverne Huntsman's body was stuck inside a lower kitchen cabinet. She wiggled her way out at the sound of Delta's voice.

"Hello," she said coolly.

Delta's cheeks turned fire engine red. She took a menacing step toward Laverne. "What are you doing?"

"I'm looking for an herb infuser. Leah showed me the herb garden around back, and I was going to try my hand at tinkering with some of the fresh herbs since I have some free time today."

"An herb diffuser?"

Laverne stared at Delta in disbelief. "You mean you don't have one?"

"Have one? I've never even heard of one."

"Well…" Laverne dusted her hands off as she stood. "It's only the most essential kitchen product on the planet. It infuses flavor into any dish."

The woman was on a roll, her spiel reminiscent of a late-night infomercial. "Who doesn't love fresh basil in their pasta sauce, or that special hint of cilantro in your salad dish, not to mention a touch of rosemary in your seafood?"

"I have something that will work just fine." Delta yanked a nearby drawer open. She reached inside and then handed Laverne a mortar and pestle.

Laverne curled her lip. "This? You want me to use this? It's antiquated. I think this thing has been around since dinosaurs roamed the earth."

"It's antiquated, and so am I, which means we work perfectly together. You can *borrow* it if you want, but I'll need it back."

"I…guess this will have to do." Laverne shut the cupboard door and lumbered across the kitchen. "I have to say, although I'm shocked you don't have a diffuser on hand, this kitchen is a dream."

"It works quite nicely," Delta said stiffly. "Jo and I designed it from the ground up."

"The kitchenette next door has everything you need," Jo pointed out. "Except, apparently, a diffuser or a mortar and pestle."

"Or a six-burner stove, a convection oven, the coffee pot is old and I couldn't find a spice rack, which is what got me started on the herb garden." She motioned to the commercial-grade six-burner gas stove that had cost Jo a pretty penny. "This baby right here is top of the line. The dinky one we have next door could barely boil water. You put the good stuff over here."

"Because this is the main kitchen," Jo patiently explained. "As I mentioned earlier, most meals are eaten here, not next door."

"Right. And like I said, I'm not sure I plan to eat every single meal here."

"We can only hope," Delta muttered under her breath.

Laverne acted as if she hadn't heard Delta's snide reply and began backing out of the room. "Thanks for the loan."

"I'll be along shortly to take you around to meet Nash and Gary and finish our tour."

"Sure." Laverne held up the kitchen utensil. "I'll return this later after I finish using it."

"You can leave it on the table." Delta waited until the door slammed shut and she was gone. "The woman hasn't been here for twenty-four hours, and she's already getting on my last nerve."

"She does seem a bit...overbearing," Jo said.

"Overbearing, opinionated, entitled. And those are her redeeming qualities."

Jo chuckled. "C'mon, Delta. I'll admit she has a strong personality, but then so do you, which is one of the reasons why I love you. Because you tell it like it is."

"Yeah, well, two loudmouths in the same house is a recipe for disaster."

"Let's play it day by day. In the meantime, I'll try to track down a mortar and pestle, or cheap diffuser for Laverne."

"Don't bother." Delta rummaged around in the same drawer where she'd found the mortar and pestle. She pulled out another, except this one was solid marble and twice the size. "I can use this one if I need to. I didn't want Laverne thinking she could sneak in here whenever she wants and start helping herself to whatever catches her eye."

"On that note, I'm going to track down Raylene. By then, Laverne should be done messing with the herbs."

She found Raylene helping a customer in the bakeshop and waited until the woman crossed over to the mercantile next door. "Hey, Jo. Where's Laverne?"

"Blending herbs and spices in the kitchen."

"With Delta?" Raylene's eyes grew wide. "They're hitting it off?"

"Not exactly." Jo grinned. "Laverne is in the common area's kitchenette, blending spices, at least that's where I think she went."

"She stopped by here earlier, looking for Delta, and then she said something about needing some kitchen supplies and planned to head next door. I tried to warn her that the kitchen was Delta's domain." Raylene waved her hand over her head. "I'm pretty sure it went right over her head."

"It did. Delta and I caught her rummaging around in the kitchen cabinets."

"And I didn't hear the fireworks from here?" Raylene joked.

"Not this time. Laverne left before it got too heated." Jo changed the subject. "I have a favor to ask." She briefly told Raylene about Wayne's surveillance camera's recording.

"Someone has been watching Sherry's apartment."

"Or Wayne's hardware store. Maybe they're scoping it out, with plans to rob it. I was thinking...I haven't talked to Sherry yet but wondered if you would be open to spending an evening or two with her, to get a feel for what's going on over there."

"Spend the night?" Raylene asked.

"Technically, it could be considered breaking a rule, but I don't see anything wrong with you spending the evening with her, which is when these incidents are occurring."

"Sure, I'll do whatever I can to help."

"Thanks, Raylene." Jo told her she would invite Sherry to dinner. Afterward, the women could return to the apartment to hang out, and then later that evening, Jo would return to town to pick Raylene up.

Her next task was to hunt down her newest resident. She didn't have far to go; she found Laverne standing at the kitchenette's counter, staring at a row of herbs. The tantalizing aroma of fresh basil filled the air.

There was a pot of boiling water on top of the stove.

"Hey, Jo."

"What are you making?"

"Pesto Italiano. It's a family recipe. I've been itching to make this ever since...my incarceration."

"A family recipe?" Jo echoed.

"It was my mother's." Laverne swallowed hard and quickly looked away. "Anyhoo, my mom made this every New Year's Eve. She never would give me the recipe, but I think I finally figured it out. It's a fairly simple mix of pine nuts, parmesan cheese, olive oil and fresh basil, blended together and then tossed in angel hair pasta."

Jo eased into an empty chair and watched as Laverne whirled around the kitchenette. While she mixed, she chatted about eating healthy, how she was excited about the herb garden and couldn't wait to check out the other gardens. "I have a green thumb if I do say so myself. Cooking and fresh food go hand in hand."

"Did you grow up on a farm?"

Laverne stopped whisking. "No. No, I didn't. I grew up in the city, but I always wanted to live on a farm."

"In the beginning, you didn't seem particularly keen on coming here, yet you're telling me that you've always wanted to live on a farm? If that were the case, I would think you would've jumped at the chance to come here."

Laverne pivoted, so she faced Jo. "It was the rumors going around. I don't want to get you all stirred up again, but some unfavorable things are being said about this place."

"And I explained why – one of the former residents took it upon herself to leave without permission, without clearing it with her probation officer. She was caught and returned to Central to finish her sentence."

"Right, and now it makes sense. I'm willing to give this place a hundred percent effort. I'm here. You seem to have a smooth-running operation. I think my being here will be beneficial to both of us."

Jo snorted. "Beneficial to both of us? I believe you need me more than I need you."

"Hmm." Laverne began grating the block of parmesan. "I know how these places work. Like any facility, it's inspected by the state. I imagine certain criteria must be met. I haven't dug into the nuts and bolts of running a group home, but my guess is you have an occupancy requirement, and only having four residents wasn't cutting it."

The woman had hit the nail on the head. There was no denying it. Jo opened her mouth to reply, but Laverne continued.

"I figured it was something like that. First, you don't want me. Then, all of a sudden, you change your mind and are hot to have me move in pronto. There had to be some motivating factor."

"Or maybe I decided to give you a chance after all."

Laverne finished grating, drained the pasta and then poured her pesto mixture on top. "This has to sit for a spell." She removed the apron and hung it on the hook near the door. "If we're heading out to the garden, I have a pair of barn shoes I'd like to change into. There is one more thing I've been meaning to take a look at before we get too far into this resident business."

Jo followed Laverne out of the common area. She stood outside her unit door and waited for the woman to swap out her shoes. Minutes passed, and Jo started to wonder if she'd changed her mind.

She reached for the doorknob when Laverne burst out of her unit. "Houston, we have a problem."

Chapter 15

"What sort of problem?"

"This." Laverne held up a white tissue.

Jo wrinkled her nose. "What am I looking at?"

"Dust. Don't you see it?"

"No. All I see is a tissue."

"My unit hasn't been dusted in weeks, and all of this dust is going to trigger an allergy attack."

"Days," Jo corrected. "I personally dusted and cleaned this unit a couple days ago."

"Well, you missed a spot."

Jo gritted her teeth and began counting to ten. "If the interior does not meet your extraordinarily extreme expectations, I suggest you clean it yourself."

"I guess I'm going to have to." Laverne carefully folded the "soiled" tissue and placed it inside her pants pocket. "This definitely does not pass my cleanliness test."

Jo refused to take the bait. "Shall we proceed to the gardens?"

"Yeah. Hang on a sec. I forgot all about my barn boots. I'll make it quick." Laverne ran inside and returned, wearing a pair of mid-ankle red rubber boots dotted with roosters.

"I like your boots," Jo said.

"Aren't they awesome? One of the kitchen staff gave them to me when she found out I was coming here and would be living on a farm."

Jo lifted a brow. "That was very generous of her."

"She owed me one." Laverne started to elaborate and then abruptly stopped.

Jo's interest was piqued. "Owed you one?"

"It's a long story," Laverne mumbled under her breath, and then changed the subject. "I can't wait to see the rest of the farm."

Jo started their tour in the herb garden, moving on to the small garden and then the larger garden. "As I mentioned before, Gary is in charge of the gardens with some input from Delta, of course."

"Of course."

Laverne made a sly comment about the condition of the plants. Determined not to let the woman get under her skin, Jo, once again, let it slide. She would have to take up her garden complaints with the chief gardener.

They finished the tour and made their way to Nash's workshop, where he and Michelle were hard at work. The introductions were brief and polite, and after they finished, they stepped outside.

Laverne fanned her face. "Nash is gorgeous. My goodness, you could create your own male model calendar with that hot hunk. I wonder if he's single."

"Unmarried and unavailable," Jo said.

"That's one lucky woman," she sighed.

"Yes, I think I am very lucky. Actually, blessed."

Laverne's jaw dropped. "You two are dating? How did you manage to snag him?"

"Manage to snag him?" Jo's eyes narrowed.

"I…I didn't mean anything by the comment. It's just that he's one fine specimen."

"Implying that I'm Plain Jane and he could've picked someone much more attractive?"

"I better shut up while I'm behind," Laverne muttered.

"Yes. Perhaps you should."

Laverne and Jo passed by the empty barn and continued walking to Gary's gardening shed. Jo gave the door a light knock before stepping inside.

A large fluorescent light burned brightly above Gary's head as he bent over the worktable. "Oh, hey, Jo." He set the seed packet he was holding on the counter and wiped his hands on the front of his denim overalls.

"Hello, Gary. Laverne and I just finished touring the gardens. They look great."

"Thanks."

Jo motioned to Laverne. "Laverne Huntsman, this is Gary Stein, gardener extraordinaire."

"Welcome to the farm."

"Thank you. You've got a fine operation set up back there," Laverne complimented.

"Thanks to Jo."

"Do you live on the farm too?"

"No, ma'am." Gary grasped his suspenders and rocked back on his heels. "I have my own place down the road."

"Gary and Delta just got engaged," Jo explained. "I'm hosting an engagement party for them this Sunday afternoon."

"You got your hands full with that one," Laverne shook her head.

"Delta's a firecracker, and I wouldn't want her any other way," Gary grinned. "I look forward to working with you. You're going to love living here."

They exchanged small talk for a couple minutes, and then Jo excused them so Gary could get back to work. "That's the end of the tour."

"Thank you for taking me around," Laverne said. "I best get back to my pot of pasta. I'll bring a sample over for you and Delta in a little while."

"I can't wait to try it." Jo parted ways with Laverne near the front of the mercantile. She found Delta in the berry patch on the far side of the clothesline.

"How's La-nnoying?"

Jo chuckled. "Her unit didn't pass the white glove test. She's whipping up a batch of her pasta for us to try. She had some tips for Gary's gardens. I think she's in love with Nash."

"In love with Nash?"

"She called him a hot hunk."

"And I'm sure you told her he was taken."

"I did. She seemed shocked we were dating and said something along the lines of wondering how I managed to snag him."

"That woman." Delta shook her head in disgust. "I hate to say it, Jo, but something tells me we're in for a long period of adjustment with this one."

"I'm afraid you're right. She also alluded to the fact that she knows I need her here at the farm." Jo rubbed her brow. "Hopefully, she doesn't try to hold it over my head."

"You best start getting the last open spot filled, just in case."

"I was thinking the same thing."

Delta followed Jo into the kitchen. "Did you talk to Raylene about her hanging out with Sherry tonight?"

"Yes, which reminds me I need to invite Sherry to dinner." Jo returned to her office, where she sent a text to Sherry, who promptly accepted and added that Marlee would drop her off as soon as her shift ended.

Laverne stopped by mid-afternoon with samples of her pasta dish. It boasted a unique freshness, and the robust Italian flavor complimented the angel hair pasta. The woman had transformed the plain pasta into a delicious dish.

Sherry arrived promptly at six and easily slipped into her old routine, helping set the table and carry dishes of food to the dining room.

One by one, the residents arrived, circling Sherry as they bombarded her with questions about her new home. The only person missing was Laverne. Jo excused herself to go hunt her down.

She found her seated on the common area's living room sofa, a large bowl of food in her lap and staring at the TV.

"Dinner is ready."

Laverne never turned as she shook her head. "I'm not up for company."

Jo crossed the room and stood directly in front of her. "You need to give the dinner hour a try."

"Maybe tomorrow. I'm not in the mood today." Laverne turned the volume up on the television as she shoveled a heaping forkful of pasta into her mouth.

"I'm not in the mood, either." Jo snatched the remote from her hand. She shut the television off and tossed the remote on the couch. "This is a non-option. You dine with us tonight."

"I'm full." Laverne lifted her half-empty bowl.

"Then sit there like a lump on a log. I don't care. What I do care is that you make an appearance."

The woman stared straight ahead, and Jo could've sworn she caught a glimpse of Laverne's lower lip trembling.

She eased onto the edge of the sofa and sucked in a breath when she noticed tears welling up in Laverne's eyes. "Why are you so dead set against having dinner with us?"

"I...I told you. I'm not hungry."

"And it's making you sad?" Jo asked softly.

"I'm not good around people." Laverne cast Jo a woeful look. "I never do or say the right thing. If I go tonight, I'm going to blow it. No one will like me."

"So, you think by avoiding the others, they won't get to know you, which means they won't dislike you?"

"Something like that," Laverne whispered. "I don't make very good first impressions."

"You'll never know until you try." Jo gently pried the bowl of pasta from Laverne's hands and set it on the coffee table. "I promise you that you are about to have dinner with the most accepting group of women...and men...I've ever met in my life. Just this once, I want you to join us. If it doesn't work out, I won't ask you again."

Laverne stared straight ahead.

Jo waved a hand in front of her face. "Laverne, do we have a deal?"

Chapter 16

Laverne reluctantly scooched off the couch. "I suppose I can agree to that. I'll try it once, and if it doesn't work out, I can eat my meals in here."

"If that's your decision, but I have a feeling you may change your mind." Jo placed the leftover food in the fridge while Laverne freshened up in the bathroom.

She joined Jo moments later, a grim expression on her face.

"Cheer up. You're not facing a firing squad. You're going to eat dinner." Jo propelled her out of the building and across the yard. She didn't release her grip until they were inside the dining room, where the rest of the residents sat waiting.

"We're sorry to keep you waiting." Jo gave Sherry a gentle hug. "I'm glad you could make it,

Sherry. We need to have a quick chat after dinner before I drive you home."

"Okay." Sherry cast Laverne a questioning glance.

"Laverne Huntsman, this is Sherry Marshall. Sherry recently moved out and now has her own apartment in Divine."

"Thanks to Jo," Sherry beamed. "I heard you're my replacement. You're going to love the farm."

"That's what I've been told." Laverne offered her a tentative smile.

"Sit here." Jo motioned to the empty seat to her left, directly across from Delta.

"The food smells delicious," Laverne said politely.

"I made a pot roast with potatoes, carrots and onions, along with a side of green beans."

"And Delta's amazing cornbread muffins," Raylene added.

"Let's pray." Jo bowed her head, and the dining room grew quiet. "Thank you, Lord, for this food on the table. Thank you for every person gathered here this evening. I pray for blessings in each of their lives. Lord, we pray a special prayer for Sherry, for her safety and her new home, and thank you for bringing Laverne to the farm. We pray the transition will be smooth for all of us, and we'll grow together as a result. Amen."

"Amen," the others at the table echoed.

Sherry was the first to speak. "You got here today?"

"This morning." The platter of pot roast passed by, and Laverne shook her head. She scooped a spoonful of vegetables onto her plate and added a cornbread muffin.

Jo watched Laverne out of the corner of her eye as she studied the others at the table. There was a lively conversation as the residents questioned Sherry about her new home and then shared the details of Gary's unexpected proposal with her.

"I thought he was choking on one of my peanut butter cream cheese truffle balls. He turned white as a ghost," Delta said. "I yanked him out of the chair and started the Heimlich maneuver."

Gary chuckled. "I thought Delta was gonna bust my ribs. I was barely able to tell her I wasn't choking."

"Next thing I know, he's on one knee and holding up a ring. It was so romantic. I'll never forget it for as long as I live," Delta breathed dreamily.

"I don't think any of us will either," Jo teased. "You mentioned a summer wedding. Have you picked a date?"

"I..." Delta cast Gary a quick glance. "We were thinking that the Fourth of July would be memorable."

"That's a great idea," Nash said. "We'll get you two wed, have a little dinner and dancing and then after dark, shoot off some fireworks out back. We'll end the evening with a bang."

The idea took off from there as the others added input on the upcoming nuptials. All the while, Laverne sat quietly, taking it in.

Raylene, who was seated on the other side of Laverne, turned to her. "We didn't mean to monopolize the conversation. It's our tradition for new arrivals to tell us about themselves."

Laverne nervously tugged on the edge of her blouse. "I don't have much to say. I got divorced years ago. A few years back, I landed a job as a live-in caretaker." She told them her employer, Geraldine, was a hard woman, but a fair woman. "Her family, they never visited much except when they wanted something. She planned to add me to her will, but never got around to it."

"Which is where your incarceration comes in," Jo prompted.

"Yes." Laverne fiddled with her fork. "I kind of added my name to her will without her permission. And I got a couple credit cards using her name."

"Ah." Raylene said. "So, you were in for forgery and theft."

"In a nutshell. Her family didn't appreciate me helping myself to her money. They hired a couple high-profile attorneys, sued me, took everything I had, probably paid off the judge and I got the maximum prison sentence."

"And now you're starting over," Jo said.

"From ground zero."

"Which is where we all started," Kelli chimed in. "The farm is your fresh start."

"You won't be sorry," Michelle predicted. "Jo is our guardian angel."

"One of several. Speaking of that." Leah motioned to Gary. "Tell them what we saw."

"Better yet, we'll show them what we saw," Gary fumbled in his front pocket and removed his cell phone. He tapped the screen and handed it to Jo. "We snapped this picture out by the fence line earlier today."

Jo squinted her eyes and studied the flash of bright light in the corner of the screen. "What is it?"

"Who is it?" Leah corrected. "Remember those two guys who showed up around Christmas and scared that woman away? Gary and I think we may have seen them."

Jo handed the phone to Delta. "I can almost see a body shape." She passed the phone to Kelli as it made its rounds.

"Leah was the one who saw them first," Gary explained. "They were big guys too. At first, I wasn't sure what to think. I snapped a picture, and by the time I put my camera away, they had just vanished."

Leah snapped her fingers. "Into thin air."

Jo had experienced a similar incident. She'd been out back in the gardens and noticed two very tall strangers near the fence and property line. She began walking in that direction and been stopped in her tracks when bright sunlight temporarily blinded her. By the time her vision had cleared, the men were gone.

"When we got over to the spot where we saw them, we started looking around, and Leah spotted this shiny piece of metal on the ground." Gary handed Jo the gold piece.

She cupped it in her hand and then passed it to Delta, who promptly bit down on its edge.

Kelli's eyes grew wide. "What are you doing?"

"Checkin' to see if it's gold. I went gold mining once, and this is how we tested the metals. The purer the gold, the softer it is." Delta carefully inspected it. "There's a mark, but I'm not sure if it's mine."

"I got me a metal detector back at the house," Gary said. "I'm gonna bring it with me tomorrow and do some exploring out back."

"Wouldn't that be something?" Jo mused. "Maybe our guardian angels are leaving gold for us."

"Angels aren't real," Laverne scoffed.

"Actually, they are," Raylene replied. "They saved me after I jumped off Divine Bridge, trying to end my life."

Laverne stared at Raylene. "You tried to kill yourself?"

"I did. Evan, a local, watched me jump. He stopped his car and ran over to help. When he got to the railing, he saw two men pulling me from the water. By the time he was able to make it down the side of the riverbank, the men were gone. I should never have survived the fall."

"But we're glad you did," Jo said. "We believe in angels. They prevented this place from burning to the ground, saved us from being robbed and, most importantly, saved Raylene's life."

"That is an interesting tale." Not knowing what else to say, Laverne reached for her glass of water.

Delta shoved her chair back. "I got mile-high lemon pies calling our names."

Jo and the others loaded the dirty dishes into a pile and carried them to the kitchen while Delta and Leah brought the pies and dessert plates to the dining room.

There was already a fresh pot of coffee brewed. Jo grabbed clean cups and the pot and began making her rounds.

Nash pitched in to help. "Laverne, has Jo assigned your work schedule yet?"

"Only for the next two days," Jo answered. "I've been a little busy."

"I want the gardens," Laverne insisted. "Either that or the kitchen."

"As I explained before, you'll have a rotating schedule. You'll be working in the mercantile, the bakeshop, the workshop, the gardens and the kitchen."

Laverne took a big bite of pie and eyed Nash with interest. "Joanna tells me you two are an item."

"An item?" Nash lifted a brow. "Yes. You could say that. We're dating."

"Huh." Laverne turned her attention to Delta. "And you and Gary are engaged, which means there's going to be an opening in the kitchen after the Fourth of July."

"No," Delta shook her head. "I have no intention of quitting my job, and neither does Gary."

"Seriously?" Laverne frowned. "I figured you would want to do your own thing."

"I am doing my own thing. This is my home, soon to be my second home."

"Hmm." Laverne sawed off another piece of lemon pie and began chewing.

Jo could see the wheels spinning in the woman's head and braced herself for what would come out of her mouth next. No wonder she was concerned about her first impression. So far, she'd ticked Delta off and scoffed at the farm's heavenly visitors.

Thankfully, Laverne didn't say anything else, other than offering to help clean up. She stuck around until the leftovers were put away and then excused herself.

Sherry grabbed a stack of coffee cups and carried them into the kitchen. "That woman is a trip."

"Got that right," Delta muttered. "She stuck her foot in her mouth so many times, she shoulda just left it there."

"It took some convincing to get her to come here for dinner," Jo began loading the dishwasher. "She told me that she's not very good at first impressions."

"Or second or third," Delta said.

"She was almost in tears."

"I'm sorry to hear that, although I find it hard to believe," Delta handed Jo a pile of forks. "She sure does put on a good act. I never would've suspected she had a sensitive side."

"Sometimes, the brashest people are the most insecure. I say we hold our opinion about the woman until we have a chance to get to know her better."

Delta mumbled.

"Delta," Jo warned.

"Okay. Fine. I feel bad she was almost bawling, but she sure has a funny way of trying to get along."

"She does seem to struggle in the social skills department." Jo turned to Sherry. "I would like to have a private word with you and Raylene."

"And I have something I would like to show you," Sherry said.

The others stayed behind to help Delta finish cleaning up while Jo, Raylene and Sherry made their way to Jo's office.

When the women were seated, Jo took her place behind the desk. "What do you have?"

"This." Sherry removed her cell phone from her pocket and switched it on. "After I went to bed last night, I kept hearing this."

Chapter 17

Sherry held up her cell phone. *Tink.*

"What is that?" Jo leaned in.

"I don't know. It started around midnight. At first, I thought it was coming from the neighbor's apartment. Now, I'm not sure."

"Can you play it again?"

Sherry replayed the recording.

Tink, tink, tink.

"Weird, huh?"

"Maybe it's pipes rattling," Raylene suggested.

"It almost sounds like something hitting the windowpane," Jo said. "Did you check around this morning?"

"Yes, and I didn't see anything."

"Raylene might be right. The building is old. There's an off-chance it was rattling pipes." Jo leaned back in her chair. "Wayne Malton caught someone on video watching the hardware store and apartments late last night."

"He did?" Sherry pressed a hand to her chest. "I knew it. I knew someone was watching the place."

"We discussed reporting it to the authorities, but they haven't technically done anything." Jo told her they noticed both her apartment lights and the neighbor's lights were on at the time.

"Do you think it was my neighbor? He has some odd habits. It seems like he's always home, but he rarely comes out until late evening."

"He is odd," Jo agreed. "I am somewhat concerned, which is why I think it might not be a bad idea for Raylene to hang out with you, at least tonight."

"Spend the night?"

On the one hand, Jo was responsible for Raylene; for all the residents. On the other hand, she still felt responsible for Sherry, as well, since she'd made the decision that the woman was ready to be out on her own.

The last thing she wanted was to put Sherry in harm's way and have something bad happen to her. Jo would never forgive herself.

"You don't have to tell anyone," Raylene said.

"You are under my direct supervision. Nowhere does it say you aren't allowed, with my permission, of course, to stay overnight somewhere other than the farm." Jo eyed the women thoughtfully. Raylene was good at sniffing out bad situations. If something suspicious was going on around the apartment, Raylene would be the first to pick up on it. "Yes. Okay. Just for tonight."

Sherry and Jo trailed behind Raylene, who ran next door to pack some things. When she returned, they climbed into the SUV.

During the drive to town, Jo cautioned the women to stay inside, not to wander out and investigate if they noticed anything.

"I have the PPD Nash gave me," Sherry reminded Jo.

"Yes, but you should only use it if absolutely necessary."

They reached Main Street, and Jo drove to the parking lot in back. She swung around, stopping near the stairs leading to the apartments. "I'll keep my phone with me tonight. Call 911 if anything happens and me if you need anything else."

"Will do." Raylene grabbed her backpack before hopping out. The women climbed the stairs, and Sherry turned back, giving Jo a small wave before they slipped inside.

An overwhelming sense of apprehension gripped Jo as the door closed behind them. She whispered a small prayer under her breath. "Please, Lord, protect Sherry and Raylene."

*****

The first thing Raylene did when she walked into the apartment was flip off the lights that Sherry had just turned on.

"What are you doing?"

"If you walk over to the window and someone is standing outside watching, they're going to see you. We need to get a visual, scan the perimeter and then close the blinds." Raylene waited for her eyes to adjust and then cautiously crossed to the living room windows which faced Main Street.

She separated the blind's slats and peered out. "Or better yet, we leave the lights off and watch."

Sherry crept up behind her. "This is freaking me out."

"Our other option is to turn the lights on and pretend nothing will happen."

"But then we won't know if someone is watching this place," Sherry said. "I can't live in fear."

"Which is why we need to figure out what's going on. Where exactly did you see someone watching?"

"Right there. Between the deli and the vacant building next door."

Raylene pressed her forehead against the glass and peered down the sidewalk. She could see dim lights coming from the vicinity of the movie theater. "Miles must be working late."

"He's there every night. Him, and some other guy."

"Other guy?" Raylene's head snapped up.

"It's one of Miles' friends. I've waited on him a time or two at the deli. His name is Chet; I don't remember his last name."

There was a thumping noise. "What's that?"

"My neighbor. He usually starts making weird noises around this time."

There was another thump. "What's he doing?"

"Your guess is as good as mine."

A hallway door slammed, and then it grew quiet. They watched as someone emerged from between the buildings. A streetlight illuminated the figure, who suddenly stopped and looked straight up.

Raylene shrank back, hoping he hadn't seen her.

"That's him," Sherry whispered. "My neighbor."

"He was looking up at us. Why would he leave his apartment, cross the street and then stare back at it?"

The women grew quiet again. The theater lights flickered, and then it went dark. The only lights on now were the streetlights.

Raylene lowered the blind and began rubbing the back of her neck. "It's quiet now."

"Yeah. I don't hear the noise tonight." Sherry consulted the clock on the wall. "Although it didn't start until around midnight."

Raylene turned the living room lights on. "Do you have your PPD close by?"

"Yeah. It's in my bedroom." Sherry darted into her bedroom and returned carrying the weapon. She handed it to her friend. "I plan to fire off a few practice rounds but haven't had a chance yet."

"I checked it out the other day when Jo and I were here." Raylene held it at arm's length, training it against the wall as she squeezed one eye shut. "This would definitely be a deterrent."

"All this staking out is making me hungry. I think I'll make some popcorn." Sherry turned the television on and wandered into the tidy kitchen.

After it finished popping, she dumped it into a large bowl and carried it into the living room. She handed it to Raylene and then grabbed their drinks.

A door slammed, rattling the picture on the living room wall.

"Todd's home," Sherry said.

"Does he always slam doors?"

"Yep. That's how I know if he's coming or going."

There was a thud, followed by a second one.

"That would drive me nuts," Raylene muttered.

"Actually, I'm starting to get used to it."

An hour passed as Sherry flipped through the television channels. "There's nothing but garbage on TV these days." She stopped when she reached a local news station.

Eleven o'clock came and went. Sherry sent Jo a text, letting her know all was quiet at the apartment except for the noisy neighbor. She set the phone on the table and lifted both hands over her head. "I'm ready to call it a night."

"Me too. It's getting late."

They made quick work of turning the couch into a makeshift bed for Raylene. After they finished, the women took turns in the bathroom.

Raylene finished last and then checked the windows and door to make sure they were locked before crawling under the covers. She lay there for a long time, staring at the ceiling. Perhaps Sherry was anxious about living alone. The neighbor next door was a little annoying, but he hadn't done anything that hit Raylene's radar other than leaving the apartment and then staring back up at it.

Her eyelids grew heavy, and she finally drifted off to sleep.

Tink...tink...tink.

Raylene's eyes flew open. She'd heard something.

Tink.

She eased the covers back and slipped off the couch, standing stock still as she listened.

Tink.

The noise was coming from the living room windows.

Raylene tiptoed across the room. She lifted the corner of the blind and peered out into the darkness.

After several long moments of studying the street and sidewalk, searching for movement, she gave up and crawled back into bed. She tossed and turned, eventually falling asleep in the wee hours of the morning. Raylene woke early to bright sunlight pouring in through a gap in the blind. She struggled to remember where she was, and then it dawned on her that she was on Sherry's sofa.

She could hear noise coming from the bedroom. Sherry joined her a short time later and found Raylene had started a pot of coffee and finished folding the blankets.

"I'm sorry if I woke you," Sherry apologized. "I'm an early riser."

"Me too. I started some coffee." Raylene followed Sherry into the kitchen. "I heard a *tinking* noise after we went to bed. I think it was the same noise you recorded the night before."

"I didn't hear a thing."

"I could've sworn it was coming from the living room windows."

"Which is where I heard it." Sherry carried her coffee cup to the window. She opened the blinds and then let out a gurgling sound. "Raylene, you need to see this."

Chapter 18

Sherry waited for Raylene to join her and then pointed to a trio of white landscape rocks on top of the shingles, mere inches from the window ledge. "Could this have been the *tink* you heard last night?"

"Yes. Without a doubt." Raylene shifted her gaze. "Someone was tossing rocks at your window."

"This is proof. This is proof someone is targeting me."

Raylene unlocked the window. She eased the screen aside just far enough to be able to scoop up the small rocks. "I think we should hang onto these."

Sherry's cell phone chimed. "Jo just texted. She's on her way here to pick you up. I have to get ready for my morning shift."

"I'll let Jo in." Raylene waited for Jo at the top of the stairs and, when she arrived, led her inside. "I think someone was throwing rocks at Sherry's window."

"Throwing rocks?"

Raylene briefly explained she'd been asleep on the living room sofa and woke to the sound of an odd noise. "I finally figured out it was coming from the living room window. When I got up to check, I didn't see anything. We found these on the roof, near the window ledge this morning." She handed one of the rocks to Jo, who held it up for a closer inspection. "I wonder if Wayne's camera caught anything."

Sherry emerged from the bedroom, which coincided with a dull thud coming from the adjacent apartment. "Not only do I have a rock-thrower, but I also have to deal with that." She jabbed a finger in the direction of the living room wall.

"We noticed the neighbor was outside last night, walking around," Raylene added.

"So, maybe he's the rock-thrower."

"We heard him come back to his apartment. It wasn't until later the rocks started hitting the window," Sherry said.

"I'm going to ask him if he heard anything last night."

"I'll go with you," Sherry met Jo near the door and joined her in the hall.

Jo rapped on the neighbor's door, but no one answered.

Not ready to give up, she leaned in. "Anyone home?" she hollered.

The door opened, and Todd Gilmore joined them in the hallway. "Good morning." His gaze shifted from Jo to Sherry. "Hello."

"Hello." Sherry extended a hand. "We haven't officially met. I'm your neighbor, Sherry Marshall."

He shook her hand. "Todd Gilmore. It's nice to finally meet you."

"We're sorry to bother you so early. Someone was throwing rocks at Sherry's window last night, and we're wondering if you had a similar incident."

"No." Todd frowned as he shook his head. "Although I did notice one of the mailboxes was damaged. I was going to report it to Wayne, the landlord, but before I could, someone had already fixed it."

"It was Sherry's mailbox, which leads us to believe someone may be harassing her."

"That's awful." Todd's eyes grew wide. "I'm sorry to hear that."

"So, you haven't noticed anything?" Jo pressed.

"No."

Jo thanked him for his time, and the women returned to Sherry's apartment, where Raylene stood waiting by the door, overnight bag in hand.

"I know you need to get ready for work," Jo said. "We'll get out of your hair."

Raylene gave her friend a hug and followed Jo out of the building and down the stairs. "We noticed the lights were on at Miles' theater last night."

"He's been working late. Since we're already here, let's see if he's around. He promised to keep an eye on Sherry's place. Maybe he's noticed something."

It was a quick walk from the apartment to the theater. The front door was unlocked. Jo called his name as they made their way across the theater lobby to the double doors leading into the auditorium.

A lone figure emerged from the reel room's stairwell. It wasn't Miles, but the man Jo had met the other day, Chet Cleaper.

"Hello," Jo greeted him. "Is Miles around?"

"Not yet. He should be here anytime. Is there something I can help you with?"

"No. I just wanted to chat with him for a moment." Jo forced a smile. "It looks like Miles is almost ready to open for business."

"We're getting close now. Pretty soon, all of our long hours will finally start paying off." The man tossed the screwdriver he was holding in the air and caught it with one hand.

"Long hours," Jo echoed.

"I don't think I've left before dark for weeks now. Lots of interesting things happen around here after dark."

A chill ran down Jo's spine. "Interesting?"

"Yes, ma'am."

"What sort of things?" Raylene asked.

The man shrugged. "Just things. They don't like new people coming around, I can tell you that."

Jo knew exactly what the man was talking about. In fact, she had to wonder if Sherry wasn't being targeted because of who she was.

"Please tell Miles we stopped by to say 'hi.'"

"Will do."

The women retraced their steps and exited onto the sidewalk.

"He's different," Raylene said under her breath. "He was giving off weird vibes."

"I was getting them, too. Marlee's place just opened." Jo nodded toward the deli. "I'm hungry. Let's grab a bite to eat."

They crossed to the other side of the street, and Jo led the way inside. "Sherry's section is over there."

They made their way to a table for two, and Jo chose the chair facing out. She caught a glimpse of Sherry, who was waiting on a man seated alone near the front. After she finished, she waved to Jo and hurried over. "You're back for breakfast?"

"We never left." Jo motioned to the man seated at the table Sherry had just left. "Who is that man? He's watching you."

Sherry gave a quick turn. "Mr. Loughlin? He's a local. He's been in here a few times now. I guess he spends his winters in Florida and then comes back here during the summer months."

"The name sounds vaguely familiar," Jo said.

"He was the mayor. He knows a lot about Divine. He even knows about you and the farm."

"Everyone within a fifty-mile radius knows about the farm," Raylene joked.

"He also knows Miles is your brother and that he bought the old theater."

"Speaking of Miles and the theater, we just left there. He wasn't around, but his helper, Chet, was."

Sherry turned their coffee cups over and began filling them. "He's the heavyset guy with the balding head."

"Yes, that's him."

"I've waited on him a time or two. He was in here the other day, asking a lot of questions. I got the impression he doesn't like Divine."

"What kind of questions?" Jo rubbed her chin. "Did he ask about you?"

"He wanted to know if I lived here in town." Sherry's jaw dropped. "I told him I just moved into an apartment above the hardware store."

Jo's scalp tingled. "Was he hitting on you?"

"I...gosh, Jo. I was so busy that day. I don't think so, but then maybe he was, and I just didn't notice."

Raylene and Jo placed their orders while Sherry jotted them down. "I'll get this right out." She slipped the notepad into her pocket. "Uh-oh."

"What?" Jo turned to follow her gaze.

"It's Nicole Brewster. She works at the Twisty Treat down the street. Great. She's heading to my section."

"You don't like her," Raylene guessed.

"She doesn't like me. I'm not sure why." Sherry hurried away and into the back while Jo continued to watch. The woman circled several tables before picking an empty one not far from them.

"Nicole Brewster," Jo said. "Why does the name ring a bell?"

"Mail." Raylene snapped her fingers. "There was a piece of mail addressed to Nicole Brewster inside Sherry's mailbox."

"You're right." Jo watched as another server approached the woman's table. She poured coffee and handed her a menu. "It looks like Sherry found someone else to wait on her."

Sherry returned to their table a short time later, carrying a tray of food. "Breakfast is served."

"That was fast."

"The daily specials are always fast." Sherry transferred the plates to the table and tucked the empty tray under her arm. "I'll be right back to refill your coffee."

"Hey," Nicole called out to Sherry as she started to walk away.

Sherry reluctantly made her way to the woman's table.

"She doesn't look happy," Raylene remarked.

"No," Jo agreed.

The woman jabbed her finger at Sherry, who shook her head. She abruptly sprang from her chair. Moments later, she stormed out of the deli.

Sherry calmly picked up Nicole's coffee cup and carried it to the back before returning to their table.

"What was that all about?"

"She was upset about the daily specials. She got mad and left."

"You mentioned her name was Nicole Brewster. Remember the other day when we discovered your mailbox had been messed with? We found a piece of mail inside addressed to her."

"You're right." Sherry shifted her feet. "I forgot all about that."

After she left, Raylene and Jo discussed Cleaper's interest in Sherry and then Nicole's abrupt departure. "I wonder if she's trying to stir up trouble," Jo polished off the last bite of her toast.

"It looks that way, doesn't it? As far as Cleaper is concerned, maybe he's interested in Sherry, but that doesn't necessarily mean he's stalking or harassing her."

"True."

The women finished their food and then headed to the cash register, where Sherry rang them up. She handed Jo the receipt. "How was everything?"

"Delicious." Jo patted her stomach. "Is Marlee around?"

"She's in the kitchen."

"I'm going to sneak back there for a minute." Jo found her friend up to her elbows in salad mix.

"Hey, Jo. Sherry told me you were here. She also told me she found some rocks on her windowsill this morning."

"Yes, and we're trying to figure out who was throwing them at her window," Jo said. "Nicole Brewster, a customer of yours, just stormed out of the deli."

"I heard." Marlee tugged on the corner of her work gloves. "It's not the first time. For some reason, she doesn't like Sherry, and for the life of me, I can't figure out why."

"Wayne told us Nicole wanted Sherry's apartment. As a matter of fact, I think she was so certain it was hers that she started having her mail forwarded there."

"She wanted Sherry's apartment?" Marlee's jaw dropped. "Oh, my gosh, Jo. I think I know why now."

"Why she doesn't like Sherry?"

"Yeah. Hang on." Marlee peeled the gloves off and dashed out of the kitchen. She returned, waving a piece of paper. "This explains a lot."

Jo studied the top of the sheet. "No kidding. I think we may have figured out who's been harassing Sherry."

Chapter 19

Although Jo could only see the top of the job application, Nicole Webster's name stood out clear as a bell.

"I never put two and two together," Marlee said. "Nicole applied for a job here a few weeks ago. I had already brought Sherry on full-time and didn't need the help. Look at the address she listed."

"This is Sherry's address." Jo started to pace. "Nicole wanted a job here. She planned to move above the hardware store, the perfect location for a downtown job, yet Wayne rented the place to Sherry instead."

"Maybe Nicole's angry because she thinks Wayne and I were showing favoritism toward Sherry."

Jo mulled over the recent incidents. Everything had happened late in the evening. Whoever was lurking nearby, targeting Sherry, had to be someone local, perhaps even someone who lived downtown. "I wonder if Nicole lives close by."

"The last I heard she was living with her mother. Her place is only a couple blocks away. I know her aunt and uncle who own the Twisty Treat. I could talk to them about it," Marlee offered.

Jo shook her head. "I'm afraid if you do, it will only make matters worse."

Sherry appeared in the ticket window, waiting while the hotline cook loaded plates and placed them on the shelf. She grabbed the food and was off again.

Marlee watched her leave. "I won't say anything for now, but if this keeps up, I think Nicole needs to be confronted."

Raylene peeked around the corner. "Are you almost ready to go?"

"Yes. Marlee needs to get back to work." Jo thanked her for the information, and she and Raylene headed out.

During the drive home, Jo told her what she and Marlee had discovered; that not only had Nicole wanted Sherry's apartment, but she wanted her job as well. "It's beginning to look like she might be behind the harassment."

"That's crazy," Raylene shook her head in disbelief. "But then again, people do weird stuff when they feel they've been wronged."

Jo had turned onto their road, and they were only a couple miles away from the farm when she noticed a red Dodge minivan following close behind. A little too close. She cast an anxious glance in the rearview mirror. "I think we're being followed."

Raylene looked over her shoulder. "You're right. Do you know anyone who drives a red minivan?"

"Not off the top of my head." Jo tightened her grip on the steering wheel and pressed lightly on the gas pedal, speeding up to put some distance between them and the tailgater. She kept the speed up until they reached the corner of the property.

The van had followed suit and sped up.

"We're almost home, and they're not slowing down," Raylene said. "You might want to turn your blinker on."

Jo flipped the blinker on, easing off the gas and lightly tapping her brakes.

The van behind them never slowed. It was almost as if they didn't see Jo's turn signal.

"They're not slowing down. We're going to make a sharp turn. Hang on." Jo jerked the wheel. The front tires squealed on the dry pavement before hitting the loose gravel drive. The SUV did a side slide.

Jo jerked the wheel to correct the slide, and they veered in the other direction.

The red minivan roared into the driveway, nearly clipping the rear corner of Jo's SUV as it flew past. The driver slammed on the brakes, gravel flying as a cloud of dust swirled around them.

"Did you see what almost happened?" Raylene gasped. "The van nearly sideswiped us."

Jo watched through the front windshield as the van's driver's side door swung open. A pair of yellow stilettos emerged first, followed by plaid yoga pants. Carrie Ford wiggled out, sunglasses covering half her face and her jaw working furiously as she chewed on a wad of gum.

She waddled across the driveway and approached Jo's driver's side door. "Joanna. I nearly took out the side of your SUV."

"No kidding." Jo pressed a hand to her chest. "Didn't you see my turn signal or my brake lights?"

"Brake lights?" Carrie tugged on her sunglasses. "Don't tell me I grabbed the wrong sunglasses again. Doggone it."

"You almost rear-ended us," Raylene said.

"You kept slowing down, speeding up."

"Speeding up, so you wouldn't run us off the road," Jo motioned for her to step aside so she could exit her vehicle. "You shouldn't be behind the wheel if you weren't able to see my brake lights or turn signal."

"I'll scoot back home and grab my prescription glasses before I finish my errands." Carrie lifted a blood-red fingernail. "I have a special engagement gift for Delta and Gary."

"You should have received my Evite for their engagement party this Sunday." Jo followed Carrie to her van, and Raylene fell into step.

"I got it. It's oh-so-clever. A tractor and wagon, and 'They're getting hitched.' I have a special gift for them. I didn't want to show everyone else up at the party. You know most engagement gifts are some sappy, sentimental doodad you stash away in a box, never to be seen again. My engagement gift is unique."

"I can't wait to see it," Jo chuckled.

"Are Gary and Delta around?" Carrie shoved her sunglasses on top of her head.

"I'll track them down," Raylene offered.

"And anyone else who wants to see what special gift Carrie has procured for our newly-engaged couple," Jo joked. "Grab Nash, and whoever else is free, so they can join in the festivities."

"I can't wait to see the looks on their faces." Carrie clapped her hands. "I was so excited I barely slept last night."

"Which is probably part of the reason why you forgot your prescription sunglasses."

Nash wandered over first, followed by Gary. "Raylene said we needed to get over here right away." He nodded to Carrie. "Morning, Carrie. You're looking particularly...festive this morning."

"This old outfit?" Carrie's bracelets jangled as she tugged on the corner of her ruffled leopard print blouse. "I was just scooter-pootin' around town running some errands. Thank you for the compliment, though."

"And almost running me off the road," Jo added.

Carrie ignored her comment. "I joined a cycling class over at the 'Y' and managed to shed most of those pesky holiday pounds." She turned to Jo. "You should try it. They're running a special, a money-back guarantee to firm your flab in sixty days or it's free."

"Are you trying to tell me something?" Jo stared at Carrie.

"I think she's one hot tamale, just the way she is." Nash playfully leered at Jo.

Kelli and Michelle emerged from the mercantile with Laverne trailing behind them. "You're back," she said.

"Yes." Jo motioned to Carrie. "Carrie Ford, this is our newest resident, Laverne Huntsman. Laverne, this is Carrie, a long-time Divine local and family friend."

"And taxidermist by trade. How do you do." Carrie offered a tentative hand. "I'm guessing you came from the local P-R-I-S-O-N."

"I did." Laverne nodded. "And I also know how to S-P-E-L-L. You can say it. You're not going to hurt my feelings. Prison. Penitentiary. Club fed. Slammer. Big house."

Carrie blinked rapidly, trying to decide how best to handle Laverne's brusque demeanor. "Yes. Well...welcome to Divine."

"I'll track down Delta." Raylene ran into the house. She and Delta joined them moments later.

"What's going on? Raylene said I was needed right away."

"Carrie has a special surprise, an engagement gift for you and Gary," Jo explained.

247

"Is it still alive?" Delta asked.

"I worked very hard putting this creation together." Carrie removed a business card from her pocket and handed it to Laverne. "Carrie's Creations. I'm always open to new business."

Laverne studied the card. "Okay. Not sure when I'll need taxidermy services, but rest assured, if I ever do, you'll be the first person I call."

"Now, without further ado, I give you my pièce de résistance." Carrie flung the van's side door open.

An overpowering stench of skunk de perfume blasted out of the interior.

Jo coughed loudly. She clamped a hand over her mouth and stumbled back. "Good grief."

"What in the world?" Nash waved a hand in front of his face.

Several of the women pinched their noses, and Laverne made a gagging sound as she stepped closer. "I don't believe I've ever seen anything quite like this."

Chapter 20

"And you never will again, I can assure you of that," Carrie primly replied.

Gary calmly plucked a kerchief from his pocket. He tied it around his face before reaching inside the van and removing a large black hawk, its wings spanned as if in flight and a laser-focused look in his eyes.

Dangling from the hawk's sharp talons was a large snake frozen in the shape of an "s," as if desperately trying to escape the hawk's grip while keeping a red-eyed rat clenched firmly in its jaw.

There was a long moment of stunned silence.

Carrie wrinkled her nose. "I didn't notice it earlier, but it does seem to emanate a distinct aroma."

"It smells like a skunk," Laverne said bluntly.

"A local farmer recovered the hawk. When he brought it to me, it was clutching a skunk. I had trouble fitting the hawk and skunk on the mount, so I swapped him out for the snake. Well? Do you like it?" Carrie beamed. "I spent all of yesterday and part of the morning working on it."

"What does it mean?" Gary asked.

"It's the circle of life. Hawks are considered good fortune. The snake represents fertility, and the rat is for good luck," Carrie explained.

"Fertility?" Delta curled her lip. "I don't need no fertility."

Gary snickered. "I kinda like it. Delta, the fertility queen."

"Bite your tongue," Delta snapped. She sucked in a breath and calmly faced Carrie. "Thank you for the thoughtful and generous gift. We will find a very special place for it at the farm," she promised.

"I knew you would like it," Carrie clapped her hands. "I can't wait for the engagement party. Have you set a wedding date?"

"The Fourth of July," Gary and Delta both answered.

"God surely had a hand in this, helping the two of you find love at your age."

"Yeah, a couple old folks crazy enough to start over," Delta joked.

Carrie gave Delta a quick hug and then Gary. "I'm sorry I can't stay longer, but I need to run back home to grab my prescription glasses before heading to my class at the 'Y.'"

As quickly as Carrie arrived, she departed. She revved up the van's engine before gunning it and careening out of the driveway. She barely slowed as she stomped on the gas and sped off down the road.

"The first thing I'm gonna do is fumigate the circle of life." Gary lifted the slab of stained wood for a closer inspection. "There's a placard on the bottom. To Delta and Gary. May you enjoy many years of wedded bliss. Best wishes, Carrie Ford."

"It's the thought that counts," Jo said. "Where will you put it?"

"In the barn," Delta said. "In the hayloft, to be exact. The smell will keep the critters away."

A carload of customers arrived and began making their way to the mercantile.

"I better get back inside to help Leah." Kelli, along with Michelle, hurried off while Nash returned to the workshop.

"I best put this thing in the truck bed to try to air it out." Gary gave Delta a peck on the cheek. "We just got our first engagement gift for the house."

"Yes, we did." Delta and Gary went in opposite directions, leaving Jo, Raylene and Laverne behind.

"Where are you working?" Jo asked Raylene.

"I'm starting my shift in the mercantile right after lunch, which I plan to skip since we had a big breakfast."

"Thanks for helping last night," Jo said. "I'm switching things up. I've decided that Laverne can train with you in the mercantile."

"I could help in the kitchen," Laverne offered.

"Did Delta ask for help?"

"No."

"Then, I think it would be best if you trained in the store."

Laverne started to say something. She took one look at Jo's stern expression and promptly closed her mouth before obediently following Raylene across the driveway.

"One day at a time," Jo muttered to herself before heading to her office.

She added a few notes to Laverne's file before turning her attention to balancing the books and then sorting through her emails.

Delta stopped by to check on her a couple hours later. "How did it go with Sherry and Raylene last night?"

"Someone is targeting Sherry." Jo explained how they'd pieced together the clues and determined it was a disgruntled potential tenant/employee.

"What's the woman's name?"

"Nicole Brewster."

"I know Nicole." Delta plopped down in an empty chair. "Her aunt and uncle own the ice cream shop. I never would've pegged her for doing anything like that, though."

"Jealousy can make people do strange things," Jo said. "I thought it was so sweet of Carrie to bring you an engagement gift."

"Might not have been something I would've picked myself, but Carrie gave from her heart, which is all that matters."

"Have you and Gary worked through your misunderstanding from last night?"

"We sure did. I'll be putting up my bright sunny sunflower kitchen curtains as soon as I finish sewing them." Delta popped out of the chair and walked to the door. "Thanks for everything, Jo. For hosting an engagement party, for always being here for me, for hiring me in the first place."

"I love you, Delta. I can't imagine the farm without you."

Delta turned to go and then turned back. "I was thinking, Laverne is here for a reason."

"Maybe she's here to teach us a lesson."

"About patience and acceptance. I got the acceptance thing down." Delta rubbed her chin. "It's the patience thing I'm a little shaky on."

"I could use a little more patience myself."

"That's all I have to say. I best get back to the kitchen."

Jo stared at the empty doorway, long after Delta was gone. Patience and acceptance. Yes, Laverne was different. She was abrasive, and Jo was beginning to think Pastor Murphy was right. She used it as a defense mechanism to protect herself so others wouldn't get too close. So they wouldn't realize how vulnerable she was.

It would take some time to find the underlying cause, to get to the rawness of wherever Laverne was coming from. Jo vowed right then and there to practice patience with her, to wait it out, to gain the woman's trust and for God to reveal the reason he'd brought her to the farm in the first place.

*****

The rest of the afternoon was quiet. Dinnertime was the exact opposite, with the residents teasing Gary and Delta about Carrie's special gift. Laverne arrived late. Jo let it slide as she took an empty spot at the table.

The others followed suit, pretending there was nothing wrong with arriving at the dinner table after the meal began, which went against Delta's number one rule...arrive on time or go hungry.

Delta cast an irritated glance at Jo. The look quickly vanished, and the conversation resumed.

After dinner, the residents were in no hurry to leave, so Jo offered to host an impromptu board game night around the dining room table.

They played Yahtzee and Scrabble and then finished it off with Jo's favorite game – Clue. The group congregated in the front yard to admire Delta's flower gardens until, one-by-one, the women excused themselves.

Nash ran next door to clean up while Gary and Delta headed to his place to hang the curtains Delta had finished sewing and find a home for Carrie's creation.

Laverne lingered behind, and Jo could tell something was on the woman's mind. "Did Raylene show you around the mercantile and explain how everything works?"

"She did." Laverne leaned against the porch post. "The women love it here. I mean, I think they do."

"Yes, they do. At least that's what they tell me." Jo motioned to the swing. "Would you like to join me? This swing has the best view in the house, and the sunsets from the front porch are breathtaking."

"Sure." Laverne followed Jo to the porch and perched on the far end of the swing. "I know you haven't asked for my advice about running your businesses, but I gotta tell you, I think the bakeshop could use some tweaking."

"What's wrong with it?"

"It doesn't smell."

"It doesn't smell," Jo repeated.

"You know, those tantalizing aromas of baked goods enticing customers to purchase your products."

"That's because Delta does almost all of the baking in the farmhouse kitchen."

"And that's another thing," Laverne said. "If I'm not mistaken, you're the sole proprietor here."

"I am."

"Well, standing on the outside looking in as an observer, it appears to me that you give Delta a lot of control. If I didn't know better, I would have said you two were partners."

"Delta is my partner. Her, as well as Nash and Gary. They don't have a financial investment in my businesses, but they most definitely have an emotional investment."

"As the sole owner, I think you need better control of your employees, that's all I'm going to say." Duke, who had followed them out, jumped onto the swing and settled in between them.

"He's a good dog," Laverne patted his head. "Dogs don't usually like me. They growl and bark."

"Duke loves everyone."

"I'm sorry if I stepped over the line in sharing my opinion. I never have been good at holding my tongue. I wanted to say thank you. Delta brought over the special soaps and shampoos earlier."

"You're welcome."

"I dusted my unit. It's a lot cleaner now."

"I..." Jo waved dismissively. "Never mind. I'm glad it finally meets your sanitation standards."

Laverne nodded. "It was nice and quiet last night. I didn't hear anything."

"The farm is a peaceful place." Jo shifted her gaze, attempting to see it through Laverne's eyes. How different it must be from a prison cell. She thought about it every time a new resident arrived...from the first days of uncertainty to the moment when it finally sank in that they had found a new home. A place where they belonged. Where they were wanted and cared for, not to mention having a family that many of them no longer had.

The farm was a place for a fresh start and a second chance. Like Sherry, a new beginning. And Emily, the first to leave.

"Curtis is a stinker," Laverne interrupted her musings.

"Talk about ruling the roost," Jo laughed. "I'm pretty sure the cat has total control next door."

"She does. I guess I'm working with Nash tomorrow."

"You'll enjoy the workshop," Jo predicted.

"I don't know if I will or not, but I can tell you one thing – it sure won't hurt my eyes to look at Nash all day."

Jo chuckled. "I'm sure it won't."

The women grew quiet, watching the sun as it sank below the field. It turned into a fiery red ball, lighting the sky with billows of pink and purple streaks.

"You were right. The sunset was pretty awesome. Don't see anything like that from a prison cell," Laverne said. "I think I'm going to like working in the gardens with Gary. He gave me a mini-tour. He loves this place too."

"He does," Jo agreed.

Laverne fidgeted in her seat and then finally stood. "I'm going to head next door. I don't want the women to think I'm being unsociable." She took a tentative step before turning back. "You're the first person who's wanted me around in a very long time. I'm not going to let you down."

"I'm glad to hear it. I have faith in you," Jo offered her an encouraging smile.

"I've been thinking about that angel thing. Do you really believe in angels?"

Jo stared at her thoughtfully before answering, remembering the dinner conversation the previous night. "I do. I believe God sends special messengers, special protectors to us, to all of us who need them, if we pray and believe, and have faith."

Laverne nodded absentmindedly. "I'll see you in the morning."

Jo watched her trek slowly across the driveway. She stopped near the edge of the building and gave her a small wave before rounding the corner.

"Our God of miracles," Jo said softly. "I believe he has one for you too, Laverne Huntsman."

Chapter 21

Nash passed Laverne on his way to the porch swing. "Care for more company?"

"The more, the merrier," Jo lifted Duke's paws to make room.

"I saw you chatting with Laverne. How's she doing?"

"Better than expected. She's trying to fit in, but she's struggling with her social skills. Reading between the lines, she has some emotional issues she's dealing with."

"Don't we all," Nash said. "How's the engagement party progressing?"

Jo told him she'd already received several RSVPs. "I think we're going to have a full house."

"I would like to offer my services, to grill out, unless you already have plans for the food."

"Food?" Jo blinked rapidly. "Good grief. I haven't even started thinking about food. I don't want to ask Delta for help. This party is for her."

"So, I take it you're on board with me grilling some burgers and hotdogs," Nash teased.

"Yes. That's a great idea. I need to get a move on."

"The barn is still clean from Christmas. You can stick with the farm theme and host it out there."

"The barn would be the perfect spot. You're full of great ideas," Jo said.

"I try. I figured between dealing with Sherry's harassment and working with the new resident, you might need some help."

The couple discussed the details of the upcoming party. The conversation shifted to Sherry's disturbing incidents. "We think Nicole Brewster, a local whose aunt and uncle own the ice cream shop, may be responsible. She wanted Sherry's apartment and her job, so we think she's harassing her."

"She'll grow tired of it and give up," Nash predicted.

"I hope so."

Gary's truck turned into the driveway. He circled around and stopped near the back door to drop off his bride-to-be.

"That's my signal to head in." Jo slid off the swing and patted her hips. "Do you think I need a workout routine to get rid of flab?"

"No way. Carrie was shooting from the lips again." Nash ran a light hand along Jo's arm. "I think you're beautiful just the way you are. There isn't a single thing I would change about you."

"Not even one?" Jo teased.

He pulled Jo into his arms and kissed her. "Well, maybe one."

Jo leaned back. "What would that be?"

"Allow yourself more free time so we can go out on real dates."

Nash had a point. The couple rarely ventured beyond the farm.

"We don't get out much as a couple," Jo agreed. "So, where are you going to take me?"

"I don't know. It looks like I need to give it some thought," Nash laughed. "And on that note, I better go." He gently kissed her one more time before reluctantly making his way down the steps and to his apartment.

After he left, Jo returned inside. She found Delta sprawled out in the living room recliner, remote in hand. "We hung the sunflower curtains. They look great."

"I can't wait to stop by to see them." Jo stifled a yawn. "Excuse me. I think it's time for me to head to bed."

Delta lowered the footrest, and Jo offered a hand as she struggled to extricate herself. "Thanks. I can't stay in this thing too long without falling asleep." She landed on her feet. "Once I wake up, I'm stiffer than a slab of wood."

"Speaking of a slab of wood, were you able to find the perfect spot for Carrie's creation?"

Delta rolled her eyes. "That thing stinks to high heaven. I told Gary there was no way we were putting it inside the house. We settled on the barn. At least the smell will keep the rodents away."

"I can't wait to see what Carrie comes up with for a wedding gift." Jo followed Delta into the kitchen. "Speaking of wedding, Nash and I figured an engagement party cookout by the barn would be perfect."

"I like that idea. What would you like me to make?"

"Nothing. This is your party – yours and Gary's. I want you to relax and enjoy it. I'm sure I can handle whipping up some potato salad, coleslaw, maybe even a pasta salad." Jo told her she'd already received a dozen RSVPs. "This will be the event of the season, until the wedding."

"You sure you don't mind hosting both here?" Delta asked. "We could always have it over at Gary's place."

"Of course, I don't mind. I can already see it." Jo made a sweeping motion with her hands. "We'll decorate with some of your favorite flowers. The wedding party will gather on the porch, and the guests will be seated in the front yard, facing you."

The women discussed the menu for the reception, which would be held immediately following the ceremony.

"I was thinking since Marlee will be handling the food, you might want to stick to finger foods...small sandwiches, bite-size burgers, a fruit plate, maybe some veggie trays."

"And some of the goodies can come right from our own garden," Delta said. "The clock is ticking. We better get a move on with planning. We'll have to make sure Pastor Murphy is available, and Marlee is up to the challenge. Course, we'll invite the same group that's coming to the engagement party."

Jo could hear the excitement in Delta's voice. "I'm so happy for you and Gary."

"It still feels like it's all just a dream, and I have to keep pinching myself. I figured I was gonna spend the rest of my days as a lonely, old spinster, living in my niece's spare bedroom until you came along."

"God had a plan, a plan for you, for me, for Gary."

"For all of the women you've helped, including Laverne," Delta said. "I watched her at dinner tonight. It's like she's got a big, black cloud hanging over her head."

"I think so too." Jo told her the two had chatted earlier. "She thanked me for taking her in…and then insulted me in the same breath about the cleanliness of her unit. She doesn't think I'm running my businesses properly."

Delta crossed her arms. "And what does Laverne Huntsman know about running a business?"

"My guess is not much." Jo chuckled. "I believe she was trying to be helpful. It just didn't come out right."

Delta made an unhappy sound. "Consider the source. Besides, you've been running this whole operation without a hitch for over a year now."

"Right." Jo almost mentioned Laverne's observation that Delta had too much control, but quickly decided to keep the comment to herself. The two had formed a truce of sorts. Opening that can of worms would only create problems.

And, if truth be told, a tiny part of Jo agreed that perhaps Delta had a lot of sway in how she ran her businesses. But if she did, it was because Jo had let her.

Regardless, Delta would never intentionally do or say anything to hurt Jo, the residents or the businesses. "I've been thinking about something she mentioned. Laverne believes if we added enticing aromas to the bakeshop, we could increase our sales."

"But the heavy-duty baking is done right here."

"As it should be, although I do believe she may be onto something."

"Huh," Delta grunted, and Jo could tell she wasn't convinced.

"It's something to think about."

The women parted ways with Jo checking both the back and front doors before she and Duke headed up the stairs to the master bedroom. While Jo swapped out her clothes for her pajamas, she thought again about some of the things Laverne had said.

Perhaps she was allowing others to control her businesses. In her defense, it was simply too much for her to handle on her own. Vowing to take a closer look at tightening up the way she ran the farm, she crawled into bed.

Jo clasped her hands and closed her eyes. She prayed for the residents, naming each one. She thanked God for bringing her to Divine and for all of her blessings.

*****

Jo woke early the next morning to the remnants of a dream about her mother. A feeling of sadness and melancholy filled her. Her dreams about her mother lingered the longest, and she knew she would be thinking about it all day.

Duke was waiting for her near the bedroom door when she emerged from the bathroom. He beat her downstairs and parked himself in front of the door, his signal he needed to go out. Jo followed him onto the porch.

Her pup bolted down the steps and promptly rolled in the layer of light dew that coated the grass. After finishing, he patrolled the yard's perimeter and returned to the porch where he did a doggie shake, pelting her with droplets of water.

"Duke." Jo shielded her face. "Stop that."

He had the decency to look guilty as he hung his head and waited for Jo to let him back inside.

Delta was already in the kitchen, working on breakfast. Jo sprang into action, whipping up a batch of scrambled eggs and frying a pan of sausage patties.

All but one of the residents joined them.

"Has anyone seen Laverne?" Jo asked.

Kelli nodded. "She said she wasn't hungry and was going to skip breakfast."

"And go hungry," Delta muttered under her breath.

"Now that you're all here and she isn't, how is she doing? Does she seem to be fitting in?"

"She's okay," Leah shrugged. "She doesn't talk much."

"She likes to tinker in our kitchen," Michelle said.

"And she's tidy," Kelli added.

Raylene was notably silent. Jo turned to her. "What's your first impression of Laverne?"

"She's different."

"Different, how?"

"I shouldn't have said anything. I don't know her well enough to have an opinion yet."

"She's obnoxious," Delta suggested. "Opinionated and bossy."

Raylene wrinkled her nose. "She does have an opinion about a lot of things, but not always in a bad way, I guess."

Jo didn't pursue the conversation and instead, began discussing the engagement party. The women offered to help Jo prepare the side dishes, and they made tentative plans to meet in the kitchen Sunday morning at eight.

Breakfast ended, and Jo helped clear the table before heading to her office. Her cell phone sat on the charger, and she realized she'd forgotten to take it upstairs the night before. She glanced at the screen and discovered she'd missed a call from Marlee.

She entered her four digit-code and listened to the brief message. "Hey, Jo. It's Marlee. I'm sorry to bother you so early, but I need you to call me as soon as you get this message."

Chapter 22

Jo's heart raced as she dialed Marlee's cell phone. Her friend picked up on the first ring.

"I'm sorry, Jo." Marlee rushed on. "I had no idea Sherry was in any real danger."

"Hang on," Jo cut her off. "What are you talking about?"

"Sherry didn't show up for her early morning shift. I went to her apartment to check on her. Her neighbor, Todd, found her. He said he heard some noises and went outside to see what was going on. He found Sherry at the bottom of the stairs by the mailboxes."

"Where is Sherry?" Jo clutched the side of the desk as she started to sway.

"We're in her apartment. An ambulance just showed up. Gotta go." Marlee abruptly ended the call.

Jo raced out of her office and into the kitchen. "Sherry's been hurt. Her neighbor found her at the bottom of the stairs. Marlee is with her now at the apartment, and an ambulance just showed up."

"I'm going with you." Delta shut the oven off and darted down the hall. She returned moments later, purse in hand. "Are you okay to drive?"

"I hope so." Jo forced herself to remain calm and took a deep breath. "I am. I'm ready to go."

It was a tense trip to town. Jo pulled in front of the hardware store, and Delta bolted from the vehicle, beating her to the sidewalk.

They took a shortcut between buildings to the parking lot in the back, where they found an ambulance parked next to the stairs.

The entrance door, as well as the door to Sherry's apartment, was wide open. Two EMTs were in the living room kneeling next to Sherry, who was lying on the sofa.

Delta and Jo joined Marlee, who was hovering off to the side. "How is she?"

"She's alert."

One of the men removed his gloves and joined the trio. "It appears Ms. Marshall suffered a mild concussion, along with a good clunk to the head. She's alert and responding. I bandaged her forehead, but she may need stitches."

The second EMT packed up his medical bag and stood. "Since she's refusing to go with us, there's not much more we can do. I suggest she get checked out by a doctor."

"Thank you. I'll make sure that happens." Jo walked them to the door and then approached the sofa. "What happened?"

"I was on my way to work this morning. When I got to the bottom of the stairs, I thought I heard someone in the alley behind me. I turned to see who it was. All I saw was a large shiny object out of the corner of my eye. Next thing I know, Marlee and my neighbor are standing over me, and there was blood everywhere."

"Everywhere," Marlee shuddered. "Show Jo and Delta your cut."

Sherry winced as she removed the icepack. Jo lifted a corner of the bandage, revealing an angry slash across her forehead.

"Were you robbed?" Delta asked.

"Sherry's backpack and work apron were on the ground next to her," Marlee said. "I put them on the kitchen counter."

Jo pressed a hand to her chest as she stared at Sherry's face. "Yes, I think stitches may be in order."

"I second that," Delta said.

"I'm sure I'll be all right." Sherry gingerly eased the icepack back in place.

"No. We're taking you to have that looked at," Jo said firmly. "Can you stand?"

"I...think so." Sherry swung her legs over the side of the couch. With Delta on one side and Jo on the other, they gently helped her to her feet.

It was a slow go out of the apartment and an even slower trek down the steps. By the time they reached Jo's SUV, Sherry was trembling.

"There's a walk-in clinic in Smithville," Marlee told them as she held the door. "Do you want me to go with you?"

"No. We can handle it from here." Jo promised Marlee she would give her an update and then drove as fast as she dared, making it to the clinic on the outskirts of Smithville in record time.

She pulled around to the front and waited for Delta to hop out. "I'll find someone to give us a hand."

Delta, accompanied by an attendant, returned moments later. He steered an empty wheelchair to the edge of the curb and helped Sherry out of the vehicle.

"I'll go park." Jo drove around the building and pulled into the first empty parking spot she found. She grabbed her purse and ran inside.

Delta and Sherry were nowhere in sight. Jo approached the check-in counter. "I just dropped off a friend, Sherry Marshall."

"She and the woman who came in with her are already in the back. Unfortunately, only two people are allowed in the examining room."

Jo thanked the woman and circled the waiting area. She took a seat in the corner and began fiddling with her phone. The minutes crawled by. At the one-hour mark, she stepped outside for some fresh air.

What if it was even worse than they suspected? What if Sherry's skull was fractured? What if she'd hit her head and there was swelling in her brain? Jo would never forgive herself.

Determined to get an update on Sherry's condition, Jo strode back inside. She was almost to the check-in desk when Delta and Sherry emerged. They made a brief stop at the front desk before joining Jo.

"What did the doctor say?"

"He stitched up my wound. I have a minor concussion. I need to take it easy for a few days."

"And have someone keep an eye on her," Delta added.

"Which means you're coming back to the farm."

"But…" Sherry started to protest, and Jo held up a hand to stop her. "I think it's best. Mother Hen Delta can hover over you. It will also give us time to try to figure out who's behind your attack."

While Delta and Sherry waited out front, Jo brought the SUV around. She joined them and helped Sherry into the vehicle before returning to the driver's seat. "I'm going to drop both of you off at the house and then return to town to update

Marlee. At the same time, I'll swing by your place to grab a few things."

At the farm, Jo made sure Sherry was settled in before heading back out. Her first stop was Marlee's deli, where she found her friend working in the kitchen.

"I was just getting ready to call you. How's Sherry?"

"She has a concussion. The doctor stitched her back together. He wants her to take it easy for a few days and then follow up with her family doctor."

"Good. I mean, not about the concussion and stitches, but that she's going to be all right. Tell her not to worry about work. I'll have some of my other servers cover her shifts," Marlee said. "Have you talked to Wayne and filled him in on what happened?"

"Not yet. I'm heading there next." Jo thanked Marlee and then crossed the street to the hardware store. She found Wayne in the fertilizers and grass seed section, helping a customer. "Hey, Wayne. I need to have a quick word with you when you're free."

"Sure. I'll be right there." He joined Jo near the back of the store after he finished. "What's up?"

"Someone attacked Sherry early this morning. When she didn't show up for her shift at the deli, Marlee came over to check on her and found her out by the mailboxes. Todd, your tenant, was with her. He said he heard a noise, went outside to check it out and that's when he found her."

"Sherry's injured?" Wayne blinked rapidly.

"She's going to be all right," Jo said. "I took her to the walk-in clinic in Smithville. She has a few stitches and a concussion. She's at the farm now, so we can keep an eye on her for the next couple of days."

"Hang on." Wayne tracked down his wife, Charlotte, who was stocking shelves near the front of the store. They had a brief conversation, and then he joined Jo. "Charlotte's covering the store so you can show me where Sherry was found."

Jo hustled to keep up with Wayne, who didn't slow until he reached the stairs. He knelt next to the steps and pointed to a trio of large, dark spots. "This appears to be blood."

"It must be Sherry's."

Wayne stood. "I'm sorry, Jo. I had no idea. I haven't had time to check the cameras this morning." They returned to the hardware store and to a small corner office.

Jo quietly watched as he turned his attention to the laptop sitting on the desk.

He tapped the keys and reluctantly shook his head. "They didn't catch anything. I'm calling the police. We need to file a report." Wayne had a brief conversation with the dispatcher and then ended the call. "Someone is on the way."

While they waited, Jo viewed the surveillance camera's recordings. Wayne was right; it hadn't recorded anyone in the vicinity early that morning.

Sheriff Franklin arrived a short time later. "Charlotte told me you were back here. Morning, Wayne, Ms. Pepperdine."

"Thanks for getting here so quickly, Bill." Wayne briefly explained what had transpired. He started with Sherry's comments a couple days ago about feeling as if she was being watched. "I set one of my cameras to record the area and caught someone watching the building."

Wayne continued. "Someone was messing with Ms. Marshall's mailbox, and this morning, she was attacked out back."

The sheriff, who had been jotting notes, stopped. "Attacked?"

"I'll show you where in a minute." Wayne replayed the recording from the other day when it caught a shadowy figure watching the building. "That's all I have."

The sheriff scribbled furiously. "Was it a robbery? Did Sherry mention if anything was missing?"

"No." Jo shook her head. "According to Marlee, who was one of the ones who found Sherry, her belongings were on the ground next to her."

"One of the ones?" the sheriff inquired.

"Her neighbor, Todd, found her first," Jo said.

"Todd…"

"Todd Gilmore," Wayne said.

"I'd like to take a look at the location of the attack."

Jo trailed behind as Wayne led the sheriff outside and to the stairs.

"Looks like blood stains here at the bottom of the steps." Sheriff Franklin lifted his hat and scratched the top of his forehead. "Has Sherry given any

288

indication she might know who's behind the attack?"

"Nicole Brewster applied for a job at Marlee's deli," Jo said. "She used Sherry's address as her own on the employment application."

"She also filled out an application to rent Sherry's apartment," Wayne added.

"It looks like I'll be stopping by the Twisty Treat to have a chat with Nicole." The sheriff clenched his jaw. "We don't need this kind of trouble in Divine. I'll be stepping up patrols. I need to speak with Sherry. Is she going to be staying here or with you out at the farm?"

"The doctor wants someone to keep an eye on her, so she'll be staying with me for a few days," Jo said.

"Do you mind if I swing by later this evening or tomorrow morning to talk to her?"

"Of course not. Although it might be better to wait until the morning to give her a chance to rest."

Jo told them what Raylene and Sherry had told her about the possibility that someone was tossing rocks at her living room window.

Charlotte emerged from the hardware store. "I'm sorry to interrupt, but I need Wayne's help for a minute."

"You go on ahead. I'm going to have a look around before I leave." The sheriff thanked Wayne for reporting the attack and promised to be in touch soon.

While Wayne made his way back inside, the sheriff circled the bushes lining the edge of the parking area. He slid his baton from the side holster and began poking around. "I think I've got something."

Sheriff Franklin pulled a handkerchief from his pocket, cautiously leaning in and then removed a shiny metal object. "I think we may have found the weapon."

Jo's stomach churned as she stared at the large metal wrench the sheriff was holding.

"It looks like there are splotches of dried blood. I'll put a rush on this at the lab." He carried the wrench to the trunk of his patrol car and placed it inside. "If we're lucky, we'll find prints."

"So, what do you think happened?" Jo asked. "Do you think the attacker struck Sherry and panicked after they knocked her out? Not knowing if they killed her, they threw the wrench into the bushes to get rid of a potential murder weapon?"

"It's possible her attacker panicked." Franklin slammed the trunk shut. "It's time to chat with Sherry's neighbor."

Jo returned to the hardware store to fill Wayne and Charlotte in on what the sheriff had found. After she finished, she borrowed Wayne's master key and made her way upstairs to Sherry's apartment. She tossed some things into an overnight bag and then checked the windows to make sure they were locked before stepping into the hall.

There was a small window, overlooking the rear parking lot Jo had never noticed before, and she made her way over.

Someone was targeting Sherry. Marlee told her the neighbor had heard noises, went outside to check it out and that's when he found her. What if it was him? What if he attacked Sherry, saw Marlee coming around the corner and tossed the wrench in the bushes?

If that were the case, Sherry was in danger.

An idea began to form in Jo's mind as she stared blankly at the parking lot. There was one way to find out who was behind Sherry's attack. Now, all she needed was a little help setting her plan into motion.

Chapter 23

Jo tightened her grip on Sherry's bag and made her way to the end of the hall. She had almost reached the exit when Todd Gilmore emerged from his apartment. "Hello, Ms. Pepperdine."

"Hello."

"How is Sherry?" Todd nervously pressed on the bridge of his glasses.

"She has a concussion and needed some stitches."

"But she's going to be okay."

"She is."

"I talked to the sheriff. He stopped by here a few minutes ago. I told him what happened, how I heard Sherry leave and then there was this noise. I could've sworn I heard someone talking, so I went to check it out. That's when I found her."

"And you didn't see anyone else?" Jo prompted.

Todd shook his head. "No. Just Sherry on the ground. I was thinking...it might be a good idea for Sherry and me – as neighbors – to exchange phone numbers. That way, if I hear or see anything, I can give her a call."

On the one hand, it would be nice to have Sherry's neighbor keeping an eye out. On the other hand, Jo didn't completely trust the mysterious man. What if he was behind the attack? "I can't give you Sherry's number without her permission, but I can give you mine for now."

"Let me go grab my cell phone." The young man hurried into his apartment, leaving his front door wide open.

Jo trailed behind. A black sofa sat against one wall. A flat-screen television was on the opposite side. A video game console sat next to the television, with a gaming chair directly in front of it.

She took another tentative step, craning her neck far enough to catch a glimpse of the kitchen. Like the living room, it was sparsely furnished. There was a small coffee pot in the corner. The rest of the counters were empty.

Todd returned moments later with his cell phone in hand. Jo rattled off her number, and then he gave her his.

"I'll be sure to pass this on to Sherry." Jo thanked him, and he followed her into the hall. "Sherry works across the street at the deli."

"She does," Jo said.

"Do you think someone from the deli attacked her?"

"I don't know." Jo paused when she reached the exit. "All I know is I plan to track down whoever did this to her, and they had better watch out."

Todd's eyes grew wide, his Adam's apple moving up and down as he swallowed hard. "I...I hope you do."

Their eyes met. Todd mumbled something under his breath before returning to his apartment and closing the door behind him.

Jo stared at the door. Although Sherry's neighbor had initiated the conversation, she got the impression he was uncomfortable talking to her.

She shook off the uneasy feeling and made her way back to the hardware store to return Wayne's keys. Since he was busy helping a customer, she gave the keys to Charlotte, who was still stocking shelves near the front.

"Please tell Sherry that we're thinking about her and to let us know if there's anything we can do." Charlotte accompanied Jo to her SUV. "And if we hear anything, we'll be sure to give you a call."

"Thanks, Charlotte."

Back at the farm, Jo found Delta outside hanging clothes on the clothesline. "How is Sherry?"

"She has one killer headache, but I think she's gonna be fine." Delta clamped a clothespin on the corner of a bedsheet. "This whole thing makes me madder than a wet hornet. We're going to get to the bottom of this one way or the other."

"My sentiments exactly. In fact, I think I have a plan." Jo briefly explained what she had in mind. "I know Sheriff Franklin is investigating, but I have a feeling even if Sherry's attacker is tracked down and confronted, they won't come clean with a confession."

"Because it's the attacker's word against Sherry's, a convicted criminal." Delta pushed the bag of clothespins along the line. "You're probably right. Well, this won't be the first time we dove headfirst into an investigation. I say we give this a little more thought before we put your plan into action."

"I agree. Sherry is safe for now, for the next few days." Whoever had done this was going to pay. Sherry had as much right to reside in Divine as the next person. She shouldn't have to live in fear for her safety.

"The doctor gave her some strong painkillers. She didn't want to take them, but I was finally able to get her to take half of one, and then she asked me to hang onto the rest."

Many of the residents who arrived at the farm were former drug addicts. Sherry was no exception. Jo could see where she would be nervous about taking prescription medications and risk becoming addicted again. "Good girl. We'll only give her as much as needed."

"And then flush the rest."

"Exactly." Jo gave her a thumbs up. "We need to make sure no one else gets their hands on them."

"I was thinking, it probably wouldn't hurt to check out some of the suspects, you know, run background checks like you do for potential tenants."

"That's a great idea."

After Delta finished hanging the laundry, she dropped the empty clothes basket by the door and followed Jo to her office. "Have you started a list of who might be responsible?"

"A mental list." Jo grabbed a pen and a yellow pad off the desk. "First on the list is Nicole Brewster. She has motive and opportunity. She wanted Sherry's job *and* her apartment."

"Nicole lives in town," Delta said. "I think whoever is targeting Sherry lives nearby."

"I agree." Jo wrote Nicole's name at the top of the sheet.

"What about the odd neighbor, the guy who found Sherry?"

"Todd Gilmore." Jo eyed her friend thoughtfully. "I ran into him on my way out of Sherry's apartment. It was almost as if he was waiting and watching for me."

"What did he say?"

Jo briefly repeated the conversation, how Todd said he heard Sherry leave, followed by another noise and then he thought he heard someone talking. "He went to check it out, and that's when he found her. He seemed nervous. I caught a glimpse of the inside of his apartment. It was neat as a pin, almost too tidy, like no one even lived there."

She added his name to the list. "There's one more. Chet Cleaper. He's the guy who's helping Miles. He's always over at the theater, which is not only close to Sherry's apartment but the deli as well."

"And he has a bird's-eye view of the deli if he's at the theater," Delta pointed out.

"Sherry also mentioned that she waited on Cleaper at the deli and told him that she had just moved in across the street." Jo jotted Cleaper's name beneath Todd's. "That's all we have, at least for now."

Delta rubbed her hands together. "Let's start snooping."

Jo opened the skip tracing site, the one she used to screen potential residents. She started with the first suspect, Nicole Brewster. She found her full name, age, date of birth, current address, a list of possible family members and past jobs. "She's worked at her aunt and uncle's ice cream shop for a long time."

"So, I wonder why she was applying for a job at the deli," Delta mused.

"To make more money?" Jo studied the screen. "She had also put in an application for Sherry's apartment. Maybe she's trying to put some distance between her and her family."

"Sometimes, family and business don't mix."

"There's nothing on her, not even a parking ticket. Who's next?" Jo studied her small list. "Todd Gilmore." She opened a second screen and typed his name in the search bar. "That's odd." Jo squinted her eyes.

"What's odd?" Delta leaned forward.

"Here's what I have on Todd Gilmore." Jo turned the laptop, so Delta could see the screen. "It's blank."

"Huh. It's almost as if he doesn't exist."

"I wonder if Wayne did a background check on him." Jo snatched her cell phone off the desk and tapped out a text to Wayne. "I'm asking him why he rented an apartment to Todd since he doesn't appear to exist."

Jo paused. "On second thought, maybe I'll ask him if he knows anything about Todd's background." She revised her text and pressed send. While she waited, she began searching social media sites.

Jo couldn't find him anywhere. He wasn't on Facebook. He wasn't on Instagram. He wasn't on LinkedIn. "There's nothing on Todd Gilmore."

"I wonder what he does for a living."

"I have no idea. All I know is he makes a lot of noise, and his apartment is almost empty."

Wayne replied to Jo's text, and she read it aloud:

"Todd was recommended by a friend of a friend. He paid six months' rent in advance in cash. Why?"

Jo tapped out a reply: "Because he has no social profile, no professional connections. It's as if he doesn't exist."

Wayne thanked Jo for the information but didn't remark on her findings. "I'm not sure if he's excited that I'm digging around his tenant's background or disturbed by my digging around," Jo joked.

"What would be Todd's motive for harassing and attacking Sherry? I mean, the opportunity is certainly there, but what's the motive?"

"Your guess is as good as mine." Jo moved on to the last person on the list, Chet Cleaper. She typed his name and Divine, Kansas, in the search bar. The screen quickly filled.

Jo started at the top. Her eyes grew wide when she reached the second paragraph. "You're never gonna believe this."

Chapter 24

"Chester V. Cleaper, Twelve Round Robin Drive, Divine, Kansas, has a Smith County criminal record."

Delta leaned in. "What kind of criminal record?"

"Willful and malicious destruction of private property." Jo tapped the screen. "I knew it. I knew there was something about that man."

"But we don't know whose property he willfully destroyed. It could be an ex, an enemy or maybe a former employer."

"Could be an innocent woman," Jo added.

"Why Sherry?" Delta asked. "I mean, if he's attracted to her, why conk her on the head? That would be an odd way of displaying affection."

"Or maybe Sherry gave him the cold shoulder. He got angry, and now he's obsessed with her." Jo rubbed her temples. "This is making my mind fuzzy."

"I gotta get hustling on lunch." Delta returned to the kitchen.

It was time to check on Laverne, but first, Jo wanted to take a walk to clear her head. Her first stop was the small garden, and then the larger of the two. She smelled the compost bin several yards away and steered clear of the area as she picked up the pace.

Jo slowed when she reached the fence line, which also served as her property line. She thought about what Gary and Leah had said about the two large men they'd seen, Gary's snapshot of the flash of bright light and how the men seemed to have vanished into thin air.

She shaded her eyes and studied the fields that belonged to Kansas Creek Reservation, a band of Indians who were Jo's neighbors on one side. She wondered how Chief Tall Grass and Storm Runner were doing.

She hadn't seen much of them lately, except during their brief visits to the bakeshop when Namid, Storm Runner's wife, stopped by to purchase some of Delta's baked goods.

Jo tucked a stray strand of hair behind her ear as the wind picked up, rustling the leaves on the trees. Was Laverne right? Was Jo giving Delta too much control?

Her thoughts drifted to the previous night's dream about her mother, and her heart ached. If only she could talk to her one more time...hear her voice, her mother reassuring her everything would be all right.

Jo blinked back the sudden tears, silently scolding herself as she forced the lingering sadness from her mind. With one last look at the empty farm fields, she returned to the front and made her way into the bakeshop.

The store was empty except for Kelli, who stood behind the counter. "Hey, Jo."

"Hi, Kelli. How's business today?"

"Slow. It was busy when we first opened, but it's been downhill ever since."

"Which sounds exactly like yesterday." Although the mercantile's business was booming, the bakeshop sales were lackluster, to say the least. It wasn't all doom and gloom, though. They were still turning a small profit, but by now Jo figured profits would be trending higher.

Jo thanked her for the update and trudged across the parking lot to the workshop. Laverne was inside, leaning on the counter and listening intently to Nash, who was showing her how to use the finishing sander. Or more like hanging onto Nash's every word.

"Hey, Jo." Nash set the sander down. "Delta stopped by earlier to tell us about Sherry's attack. I can't believe it."

"The good news is she's going to be all right." Jo told him Wayne had called the police and reported the incident. "Sheriff Franklin is investigating. In the meantime, Sherry is staying at the house and is under Delta's watchful eye." She motioned to Laverne. "How's it going with the new trainee?"

"Great," Laverne clasped her hands. "I never thought woodworking would be so interesting. Of course, it *could* be because of the teacher."

Jo laughed. "Yes, I'm sure it could be." Laverne wasn't the first resident to flirt with Nash, a former army man.

His eyes twinkled with mischief. "Maybe you should spend the day with me here in the workshop, and I could teach you a thing or two."

Jo's heart did a flip-flop as their eyes met. Nash's hair had grown out, forming small ringlets that framed his face. He was spending more time outdoors now that the weather was nice and was sporting the beginning of a golden summer tan. His muscles, sculpted from years of working around a farm, bulged beneath his fitted t-shirt.

Laverne watched the exchange with a great deal of interest. "You two really are digging each other."

"Yes," Nash grinned. "We dig each other."

Jo cleared her throat. It was time to shift the conversation to a safer topic. "The bakeshop business is a little lackluster lately."

"You mean as far as sales?" Nash asked.

"Yes. Maybe it's a late spring, not-quite-summer slump." Jo waved dismissively. "I didn't come here to complain. I just wanted to pop in to see how Laverne was doing."

Jo returned to her office and checked her email, where she found another round of RSVPs. She ran the numbers and counted over two dozen friends and family who planned to attend the engagement party.

She spent the rest of the afternoon in her office and made it through dinner before excusing herself and turning in early. She fell fast asleep and woke early to the clanging of pots and pans echoing up through the register ducts.

When she reached the kitchen, she found Delta already hard at work. "Looks like we're falling into a new routine – up before the rooster crows."

Jo poured a cup of coffee. "I can't stop thinking about Sherry's attack. I've decided to move forward with my plan."

"Which is…" Delta prompted.

"To hide out in her apartment. We wait for her attacker to strike again and then BAM!" Jo smacked her hands together. "We take them down."

Delta refilled her coffee cup and joined Jo at the kitchen table. "And how do you propose we take them down? Shoot them?"

"I haven't got that far yet."

"Well, I have. I say we Byrna them."

"Burn-a them?"

"The PPD Nash bought for Sherry. He has one too. I was thinking we could borrow it and do a little target practice. It's been a while." Delta tapped the side of her forehead. "Thinkin' and shootin' go hand in hand. As soon as breakfast is over, we can head out back. By the time we finish, we'll have worked out the details."

During breakfast, Delta asked Nash about borrowing his PPD. "We're thinking we need to do a little target practice. Besides, if I like your Byrna, I might have to break down and buy one for myself."

Nash lifted a brow and turned to Jo. "And you're going to shoot it too?"

"Sure." Jo shrugged. "Why not?"

After clearing the kitchen, Delta and Jo stopped by the workshop, where Nash gave them detailed instructions on shooting and handling the PPD.

Jo figured Delta, who was somewhat of a weapon's expert and owned a small arsenal, would pooh-pooh him. Instead, she carefully listened to everything he told her.

"Thanks, Nash." Delta reached for the Byrna. "I did some research. This baby fires off pepper rounds too. Mind if we try a couple?"

"Not at all. You'll need these." Nash reached into the cabinet behind him, pulled out two full-face masks and handed them to Jo. "I would strongly advise wearing these if you plan to fire off pepper rounds."

"Will do." Delta led the way out of the workshop and closed the door behind them. "You ready for this?"

"Yes, ma'am," Jo rubbed her hands together. "Let's go fire off some pepper spray."

Chapter 25

The women made their way to the backyard, where Delta had already set up a makeshift target.

"You're prepared," Jo joked.

"You bet. I did a little research and discovered this baby is almost as powerful as a twenty-two." Delta held the gun at eye level, squeezed one eye shut and trained it on the target. "We can switch it up between the pepper spray and the projectiles. I suggest we start with the projectiles. If not, we might end up gassing ourselves."

Delta fired off a few shots before handing it to Jo, who completely missed her target the first time.

"Don't be shooting willy-nilly. You gotta focus."

"I thought I was. It's been a while." Jo took her time, studying the bullseye before pulling the trigger. Her second shot made it to the second ring.

"Much better." Delta patted her back. "We can recycle the ones that missed the mark."

"Meaning my shots."

The women searched the target area and managed to salvage a few of the projectiles. The more Jo practiced, the more comfortable she became with the PPD, and the better her aim.

"Looks like we have the projectile part mastered. Are you ready to move on to the pepper spray?" Delta handed Jo one of the masks.

"As ready as I'll ever be." Jo adjusted her mask and watched while Delta swapped out the projectiles for the pepper spray rounds. She fired off the first one. It splattered against the target, creating a wisp of smoke that quickly dissipated.

Disappointed, Delta lowered the gun. "Where's the explosion? I thought there would at least be a cloud of smoke."

"Maybe it needs to hit a hard surface to explode."

"Right." Delta darted to the target. She pulled the pile of straw and the target away from the fencepost and ran back.

She fired a second pepper spray projectile. The result was the same – a *pop,* followed by a small puff of smoke. "I guess that's all we get." She handed the gun to Jo. "You try it."

Jo shot at the fence post, and there was a second pop and puff of smoke. The women each fired off a few rounds until there was a thick cloud of smoke hanging in the air.

"That was fun." Delta peeled off the mask. She made a gagging sound and doubled over as a plume of pepper spray drifted toward them.

"Now I know what I'm buying you for Christmas." Jo gasped for air. She fanned her face as her eyes started to burn. "We better get out of here."

The women grabbed their things and made a hasty retreat, stopping by the workshop to return the borrowed gun and safety equipment.

"Well? How was it?" Nash asked.

"It was fun." Delta jabbed her finger at Jo. "We were able to recycle some of the projectiles when, ahem, someone missed the target the first few times."

"Practice makes perfect," Jo quipped. "Thanks for the use of the equipment. As soon as Sherry is feeling better, I think she could use a little practice too."

"Before you go," Nash stopped Jo. "Are you going to be around this afternoon?"

"I am. Why?"

"I have a surprise for you. It should be arriving any time now."

"A surprise? What is it?"

"I can't tell you. You'll have to wait and see." Nash smiled, the dimple in his chin deepening.

"And I helped," Laverne chimed in.

"She did."

"I can't wait." Jo's next stop was to check on Sherry. Her bedroom door was ajar, so Jo eased it open and stuck her head around the corner. "Good morning."

"Morning, Jo."

"May I?"

"Sure."

Jo slipped inside the room. "How are you feeling?"

"Other than a little headache, much better. I'm ready to go home."

"I'm sure you are." Jo perched on the edge of the bed. "Marlee isn't planning on you returning to

318

work until Monday. I would like you to stay here for another day or so until we can figure out who attacked you."

"I've been thinking about the attack. There's something else. There was something about my attacker." Sherry clutched the sheets to her chest. "It's there. I just can't remember."

"You took a good clunk to the noggin'. Try not to force it." Jo patted her leg. "I ran into your neighbor, Todd, this morning. He seemed very concerned about you. We exchanged cell phone numbers. I think he feels bad about what happened."

An uneasiness settled over Jo as she thought about how it had seemed as if Todd had almost been waiting, watching for her.

"You don't think he's responsible, do you?"

"I'm not certain." Jo thought about the list of possible culprits – not only Todd but Chet Cleaper and Nicole Brewster. She wondered how the sheriff's conversation with Nicole went.

There was a light rap on the bedroom door, and Delta appeared. "Sheriff Franklin is downstairs. He's here to chat with Sherry."

"Are you up to talking?" Jo asked.

"Sure. Let me change, and I'll be right down." Sherry slid out of bed, grabbed her backpack and hurried out of the room while Jo and Delta returned downstairs.

The sheriff stood near the door, hat in hand. He cast Jo an apologetic smile. "I hope I haven't caught you at a bad time."

"No, not at all. Sherry will be down shortly," Jo said. "Were you able to verify the wrench was the weapon used in her attack?"

"Yes, ma'am," the sheriff nodded. "We were. The attack was carefully planned out."

"How so?" Delta asked.

"The wrench was clean."

Jo's heart sank. "So, there weren't any prints on it."

"None, except for a small one near the base," the sheriff said. "Unfortunately, the fingerprint doesn't match anyone in our database."

"Which means the perpetrator doesn't have a criminal record." That knocked Chet Cleaper, who had a record, off the list.

"Correct."

The trio made small talk until Sherry joined them.

He politely inquired about her health and then asked her about the recent string of events.

Sherry told him how she noticed someone across the street and then mentioned the damage to her mailbox. "I think someone was throwing rocks at my window too."

"Throwing rocks?" the sheriff paused, his pen mid-air.

"They're white."

"I mentioned it to you yesterday," Jo reminded him. "They're the kind used for landscaping."

"Yes, you did. I see that in my notes now." The sheriff tapped the top of his notepad with the tip of his pen. "Tell me what you remember about the attack."

"It was early yesterday morning. I was leaving to head to work at the deli. It was around seven, and still kinda dark out. I was in a hurry and not paying attention." Sherry told the sheriff that when she got to the bottom of the stairs, she stood near the corner of the building, checking to make sure she had her work apron and money.

"Money?" the sheriff interrupted.

"I save up my cash tips and then once a week, on Thursdays, I walk to Divine Savings and Loan down the street and deposit the money."

"Every week," the sheriff repeated.

"Yes."

"How much cash do you deposit? Is it a substantial amount?"

"To me, it's substantial. Some of my tips are included in the credit card transactions, but about half are in cash."

"Give me a rough estimate of how much cash you carry around."

Jo interrupted. "Do you think it's possible someone has been watching Sherry, knows she has cash and planned to rob her?"

"I'm not ruling anything out. The only problem with that theory is Sherry wasn't robbed. Marlee said Sherry's backpack and belongings were on the ground next to her."

"Maybe they panicked after they knocked her out, tossed the weapon and then ran off," Jo theorized. "Or, maybe Todd, the neighbor, scared them away."

"It's possible. Then what happened?"

"I saw a large shiny object out of the corner of my eye. Next thing I know, Marlee and my neighbor are standing over me, and there was a lot of blood."

"Can you think of anything else?"

Sherry shot Jo a quick look. "I told Jo there's something else, but I can't remember what it was." She pressed a light hand to her temple and winced. "It's making my head hurt."

"I think I've asked enough for now." The sheriff placed his hat on top of his head. "Thank you for talking with me."

"Why don't you head back to bed?" Jo gently suggested.

Sherry returned upstairs, and Jo waited until she heard the bedroom door close. "Have you had a chance to chat with Nicole Brewster?"

"I have."

"And?"

The sheriff shook his head.

"Is she still considered a person of interest?" Jo persisted.

"As a matter of fact, she is."

"Any others?"

"Yes, there are others."

Jo followed him out onto the porch. "I'll let you know if Sherry remembers anything else."

The sheriff thanked her before climbing into his patrol car and driving off. She reached for the door when she heard someone calling her name. Nash stood near the workshop, motioning to her.

She changed direction and headed his way. "Hey, Nash."

"I saw the sheriff leave. Did he talk to Sherry?"

"He did. Sherry told him everything. She said there's something else, but she can't remember what it is."

"She took a pretty good whack to the back of her head," Nash said. "By the way, your surprise is ready."

"Surprise?"

"Remember when I said I had something for you?"

"I do...now." Jo tapped the side of her forehead. "There's so much going on, I have no idea if I'm coming or going."

Nash led her into his workshop. "Stay right here. I need to check a couple things first. I'll be right back." He exited out the side door and closed it behind him.

Jo peered out the window and watched as he strode into the bakeshop. He emerged moments later and made his way back inside. "I'm ready."

"Where's Laverne?"

"You'll find out in a minute." Nash dangled a bandana. "I need to blindfold you first." He tied the blindfold across Jo's eyes and then checked for gaps. "Can you see anything?"

"Nope. Nothing."

"Great." Nash held Jo's arm and placed a light hand on her back as he guided her out of the workshop.

Gravel from the driveway crunched underfoot. They continued walking. A door opened, and she could feel a cool draft of air blast her in the face. There was something else. It was the smell of cinnamon and vanilla.

Jo could hear the low murmur of voices. Nash led her several steps forward and then stopped. "This is it." He slid the bandanna off her head, and Jo opened her eyes.

Chapter 26

"It's an oven." Jo stared at the compact three-burner unit.

"You said bakeshop sales were down. What better way to drive sales than to create the perfect buying environment?" Nash said. "I can't take all of the credit. After you mentioned the bakeshop sales slump, Laverne and I got to talking."

"I told Nash people buy with their senses," Laverne picked up. "They'll get one whiff of those decadent, tasty treats and won't be able to resist."

"We talked about this the other night," Jo patted Laverne's arm. "It is a great idea. I'll be curious to see if this works and if it increases sales."

"What did I miss?" Delta barged into the bakeshop. "I heard something about a surprise for Jo."

"This." Jo pointed to the oven. "Nash bought a small oven to bake some tasty treats and create a buying environment."

Delta pursed her lips. "You're gonna start baking out here?"

"Not whipping up batches of baked goods, but perhaps we could try aromatizing this place." Jo warmed to the idea. "It can't hurt. If the smells don't entice people to buy, nothing will.

"Hm." Delta frowned at the small oven. "How much did that set you back?"

"Delta," Jo chided. "I think it's worth a try."

"It was partly my idea," Laverne chimed in.

"If it doesn't work out, we can always move this new oven into the common area to replace the old one," Nash said.

"I think we should have one like Delta's," Laverne said.

Jo shot her a warning look.

"Fine. Forget a new oven for us poor, neglected residents."

"Poor, neglected residents?"

"Mark my words," Laverne wagged her finger. "This is gonna work like gangbusters."

A trio of women crossed over from the mercantile to the bakeshop. "Something smells good. We had to come over to check it out."

Laverne shot Delta a triumphant look, to which Delta rolled her eyes and marched out.

Jo, Nash and Laverne followed behind, giving the customers ample room to peruse the bakeshop's display cases.

"Thanks, Laverne...and Nash. I can't wait to see if it works." As they stood chatting, the women who were in the bakeshop exited the store carrying boxes of baked goods.

"Mmm...hmm," Laverne lifted an eyebrow.

"C'mon." Nash nudged Laverne toward the workshop. "There's such a thing as tooting too much of your own horn."

Jo shook her head and watched them go. It was time for her to inventory the items needed for the party. Her first stop was the cellar, where she found bags of potatoes for the potato salad, cabbage for the coleslaw and onions for the hamburgers and hot dogs.

She placed the produce on the kitchen counter and rummaged through the fridge, inventorying the contents for the rest of what was needed, which is where Delta found her a short time later.

"Whatcha doing?"

"Inventorying items for Sunday's big shindig."

"You sure I can't help?"

"This is your party. I want you to be able to sit back and enjoy it. Besides, I'll have plenty of help from the women."

"Even Laverne? I don't want her getting too comfy in my kitchen."

"Even Laverne. You're going to have to let her in here sometimes. Besides, we've already established the ground rules. She knows what she can and cannot do." Jo finished her list and grabbed her keys. "I'm going to swing by Marlee's place after I'm done shopping and give her an update on Sherry."

"Can I go?"

Delta and Jo turned to find Sherry standing in the doorway. "I want to pick up some extra clothes for Sunday's party and check on my place."

"Yes. Of course," Jo said. "You're not a prisoner here. Although I need to pick up a few groceries for the party, it shouldn't take long."

"Let me go grab my backpack."

When Sherry returned, she and Jo headed out. Their first stop was the county's superstore, where the two of them walked the aisles, gathering the items on Jo's list.

They filled the rear of the SUV and drove to Sherry's apartment. "Whose vehicle is that?" Jo motioned to a brown Jeep in the parking lot.

"It belongs to Todd." Sherry climbed out of the vehicle and joined Jo near the bottom of the stairs. "I've been wondering...do you think whoever attacked me lives nearby?"

"I do."

"Which means I probably know them," Sherry said.

"I don't think you're being randomly targeted." Jo shifted her feet. "Other than Nicole, have you had any sort of incident with a deli customer recently, something that may have set someone off?"

Sherry shook her head. "No. Not off the top of my head. Most of the customers are very nice."

Inside the apartment, Sherry made a beeline for her bedroom while Jo drifted to the window. She gazed at the deli across the street. It would be easy for someone to track Sherry's schedule. Ninety percent of the time, she was either working or at home.

Whoever it was, was keeping tabs on her. But why attack Sherry? Money wasn't the motive. Her attacker had left her belongings intact. There had to be another reason.

It was still possible Nicole was the culprit, angry and bitter about Sherry's job and her apartment. Perhaps she was trying to scare her into quitting and moving back to the farm, leaving an opening for both the job and the apartment.

Or maybe it was Chet Cleaper. He started helping Miles right around the time of Sherry's first incident when she noticed someone lurking. The theater was only steps away from her apartment.

It would be easy for him to slip around back. Cleaper also had a criminal record.

And then there was Sherry's neighbor, Todd, who was the exact opposite of Cleaper with no traceable history. It was almost as if the man didn't exist. Not to mention that he'd paid his rent upfront and in cash.

"I'm ready. I heard you and Delta talking. Are you going to come back here tonight to see if anything happens?"

"I don't know. Obviously, your attacker knows they hurt you. Do you think they would be brave enough – or stupid enough – to return here?" Jo was on the fence. On the one hand, she was willing to give it a shot. On the other hand, there was a good chance nothing would happen, and they would be wasting their time.

They swung by the SUV to drop Sherry's things off and then tracked down Marlee, who was in the deli kitchen assembling sandwiches.

She caught sight of Sherry and hurried over. "Sherry. How are you feeling?"

"Better. My head doesn't feel like it's going to explode anymore. It's more of a dull hammering."

"I'm glad to hear you're on the mend." They discussed Sherry returning to work Monday morning. "Have you gotten an update from the sheriff?"

"Not yet," Jo answered. "He stopped by the farm earlier to talk to Sherry."

"There's something about the attack I can't remember." She pressed her fingers to her forehead. "I had hoped that stopping by the apartment would jog my memory, but so far, no luck."

"You take care of yourself and rest. Mr. Loughlin asked how you were doing yesterday morning when he came in. He said he hopes you're feeling better soon."

"That was nice of him." Sherry wrinkled her nose. "Believe me, I'll be more than ready to return to work."

Marlee accompanied them to the door. "We miss you, but don't want you back until you're completely recovered. As far as Sunday's party, do you need help with the food?"

"No. Thanks for the offer." Jo rattled off the menu. "Nash is grilling burgers and hot dogs, and I'm making some salads. Sweet tea, sodas and cookies are on tap. The simpler, the better."

"Sounds like you have it under control." Marlee gave Sherry a small hug. "I'm glad to see you doing better."

"Thanks, Marlee. Thanks for finding me. I need to thank Todd too."

"Don't ever scare me like that again." Marlee wagged her finger.

"Believe me, I don't plan to."

Back at the farm, Sherry excused herself to go lie down while Delta helped Jo unload the groceries. "Did you find out anything new?"

"Nope. Nothing. Sherry still can't remember. I've decided it won't hurt to run by her place later to scope it out."

"Then I'm going with you," Delta said.

During dinner, Jo and Delta shared their plan to hang out at Sherry's place to see if anyone showed up.

Gary was dead set against it. "You're putting yourself in harm's way."

"I've been putting myself in harm's way for decades now. I got my own way of doing things," Delta said. "Right now, we gotta figure out who's targeting poor Sherry."

"I have to agree with Gary," Nash said. "Maybe we should go with you."

"I appreciate the offer, but I'm almost certain that Delta and I aren't in any danger. We're not the target." Jo shrugged. "If nothing happens, it could be as much of a clue as something happening."

"Because whoever it is, is keeping close tabs on Sherry."

"Exactly."

Nash sighed heavily. "I recognize the look in your eyes. I can see that no matter what I say, you aren't going to change your mind."

"You know me so well." Jo blew him a kiss.

"We'll be protected by my Smith and Wesson," Delta said.

"Don't do anything foolish. If you see something, call the cops," Gary said.

Delta squeezed Gary's hand. "It's nice to have someone worry about me. You have my word; we're not going to do anything foolish."

"At least not intentionally," Jo joked.

After the men left, Jo headed to the SUV while Delta grabbed her gun. When she caught up, Duke was with her.

Delta opened the back door and waited for the pup to climb inside. "Figured old Duke and his keen senses might come in handy."

"Good idea."

Duke scrambled to the center of the seat and positioned himself so that he had an unobstructed view out the windshield.

There were few cars parked downtown since most businesses had closed for the evening. The lights from Claire's laundromat blazed brightly, and Jo could see several people inside. She turned the corner and pulled into the apartment's parking lot.

"We don't want to park here," Delta said.

"You're right. This vehicle is a big red flag." Jo circled the block and then pulled into an empty spot not far from the laundromat.

As soon as Jo opened the back door, Duke bolted.

"Duke. Get back here right now!"

The pup, who had made it to the other end of the street, galloped back to Jo's side.

"That's better." Jo clipped his leash to his collar and gave it a gentle tug. "You're free to roam the farm, but we're in unfamiliar territory and I need to keep an eye on you."

The dog gave her an exasperated look before becoming distracted by all the new sights and smells. Up ahead, Jo noticed the lights from the theater beamed off the sidewalk. "Looks like either Miles or Chet is working late again."

They took a shortcut between the buildings and then silently crept up the stairs to the apartment entrance.

"I don't want Todd to know we're here." Jo quietly eased the door open, and the women tiptoed to the other end. She didn't let out the breath she was holding until the door shut behind them. "Let's close the blinds before we turn on the lights."

"Good idea." Delta waited for Jo to close the blinds before flipping the light switch. "Now what?"

"We wait."

The women settled onto the couch while Duke patrolled the apartment. He returned a short time later and flopped down on the floor near Jo's feet. "Maybe we should turn the television on and make some noise." She switched the television on and turned the volume up.

Half an hour passed, and then an hour.

Delta wiggled off the sofa and stepped over to the window. She lifted the corner of the blind, peering out. "I feel like we should be doing something."

"We are. We're waiting."

"This is boring." Delta made her way into the kitchen and began straightening the contents of the cupboards.

Duke lifted his head and lowered his ears as he let out a low warning growl.

Jo muted the television. "What is it, Duke?"

There was a sharp rap on the front door, and Jo jumped. "Someone is here."

Duke barked loudly and ran to the door, positioning himself directly in front of it.

"Who could be knocking at this hour?" Jo crept across the room and peered out the peephole at the person standing on the other side.

There was another rap, louder this time.

Jo led the pup away from the door and joined Delta in the kitchen. "It's the neighbor. Now, what do we do?"

Chapter 27

"We don't answer the door," Delta whispered back.

Todd Gilmore knocked again.

Duke barked a reply.

"Sherry. It's me, Todd." A male voice echoed from the hallway.

Delta pressed a finger to her lips and shook her head.

He knocked a third time, and then it grew quiet.

Jo braced herself, half-expecting him to bust the door down, but nothing happened. She stood still for several long moments before tiptoeing to the window. The mercury light cast long shadows along the sidewalk.

She thought she caught a glimpse of someone standing off to the side. Jo blinked, and when she looked again, the spot was empty. "I must be tired. I think I'm starting to see things." She took a step back, lifting both hands over her head as she yawned.

"This was a bust," Delta emerged from Sherry's bedroom. "It's after midnight. Nothing is happening."

"Let's head home. Sherry forgot a couple things. I'm going to grab them before we go." Jo gathered her belongings and waited for Delta to join her by the door. She grasped the handle as she peered out the peephole. "You're never gonna believe this." She stepped aside, making room for Delta.

Delta squinted one eye as she stared out. "The neighbor's door is open. He's keeping an eye on the place."

"Which is what he promised me he would do," Jo groaned. "Now what?"

"We leave." Delta swung the door open and stepped out of the apartment.

Jo flipped the lights off. She coaxed Duke into the hallway before pulling Sherry's door shut behind her and then checking to make sure it had locked.

Todd appeared in his doorway. "Hello."

"Good evening, Todd."

"I..." He shook his head, confused. "I thought Sherry was home. I heard a dog barking."

"It was just us." Jo patted Duke's head. "We stopped by to grab a few of Sherry's things and brought Duke along for protection." She lifted the bag of clothes she was holding as she made her way to the exit.

Todd followed behind. "I've been keeping an eye on the place. When is Sherry coming back?"

"We're not sure quite yet," Jo vaguely replied.

"I see. Well, I heard noises and thought I should check it out."

Jo thanked him and waited for him to return to his apartment and close the door before leading the way out of the building.

They reached the bottom of the stairs, and Delta shivered as she eyed the dark parking lot. "I get the feeling someone is watching us. Wayne needs to add more lights out here."

"No kidding." Jo's eyes squinted as she peered into the darkness.

Delta reached inside her pocket and pulled out her handgun. "You got that flashlight?"

"Yes." Jo tightened her grip on Duke's leash as she switched her flashlight on.

The women let Duke lead the way, staying close together as they crept forward, shining the flashlight along the bushes and into the dark corners.

When they got to the sidewalk, they turned right, walking at a brisk pace until they reached Main Street. Miles' theater, which was now dark, was to their left.

The only sound was the echo of a rooftop a/c unit. They walked to the end of the block, past the hardware store. The laundromat and Jo's SUV were in sight and across the street.

"Maybe we're being paranoid," Jo unlocked the doors, letting Duke inside first. She switched the flashlight off and climbed behind the wheel. "There's only one thing that struck me as even remotely suspicious."

Delta joined her. "The neighbor, who went from suspiciously secretive to suspiciously concerned."

"Exactly. Three days ago, I could barely get him to answer his door. Now we can't get him to close it," she joked.

"I call tonight's stakeout a total waste of time," Delta sighed. "We aren't any closer to figuring out who's behind all of this."

"It's not Chet Cleaper. Remember Sheriff Franklin said they ran the print they found on the wrench and couldn't match it to anyone."

"Unless..." Delta lifted a finger, "the wrench belonged to someone else. He stole it and was wearing gloves at the time of the attack. I mean, if you had a criminal record and were about to attack someone, wouldn't you make sure you were wearing gloves?"

"True." Jo stared at Delta. "What if it was him, he borrowed Miles' wrench, waited for Sherry to come out of her apartment the other morning and then attacked her?"

"We still need motive," Delta said. "There's also Nicole Brewster."

"And now the secretive turned nosy neighbor. Three possible suspects, but only one with a clear motive." Back at the farm, they found Sherry in the kitchen, seated at the table, doodling on a pad of paper. "How did it go?"

"It was a bust." Jo handed Sherry her keys and the bag of clothes. "Nothing happened."

"Your neighbor has come out of his shell," Delta patted Sherry's shoulder. "He was looking for you earlier. He said he's keeping an eye on the place."

"That's weird, I mean, it seems out of character from what little I know of him."

"We thought the same thing." Jo kicked off her shoes. "We figured you would be in bed by now."

"I was worried about you," Sherry said. "Plus, remember when I said there was something in the back of my head and I couldn't remember? Well, I remember now what it was."

Chapter 28

"My attacker said my name. He said, 'Sherry.'"

"He?" Jo repeated.

"It was a guy's voice. I heard someone call my name. Next thing I know, I'm flat on my back, and Todd and Marlee are standing over me."

"That takes Nicole off the list," Delta did a thumbs down.

"Leaving Todd, your rescuer or maybe attacker, and Chet Cleaper." Jo tapped the tip of her chin. "It's someone who knows you, someone who knows where you live and knows your schedule."

"Which could be the neighbor," Delta pointed out.

"Or Chet Cleaper, who has been working at the theater for several days now, but why him – or for that matter, why the neighbor, Todd? What motive would either of them have?"

"Or anyone else," Delta said. "Sherry hasn't done anything. The only person who even remotely had a motive was Nicole."

"So, maybe she hired someone to attack Sherry for her," Jo theorized.

"It's possible."

"What you remembered is significant. Unfortunately, I'm not sure how. There's something that's smacking me in the face, so close I can't even see it," Jo shook her head. "Maybe once I get a good night's sleep, it will come to me."

Sherry turned in first, and Delta and Jo weren't far behind.

It was during the middle of the night when Jo woke that she realized what had been troubling her.

It took a long time for her to fall back asleep. Right before she did, she vowed to drive to town in the morning to confirm her suspicions.

*****

It was still dark when Jo stumbled out of bed and headed to the bathroom. She flew through her morning routine in record time.

Since it was still early and not wanting to disturb Delta, she made her way to her office to get some work done.

Several more Evite confirmations had arrived, bringing the number of guests planning to attend Delta and Gary's engagement party to almost thirty, not counting Jo, Nash and the farm's residents.

She also had an email from Pastor Murphy, inquiring about her new arrival. Jo drafted a reply, telling him that so far, so good. She finished the email but didn't hit "send" as she contemplated her response.

Laverne's arrival had taught Jo a valuable lesson. Although first impressions were important, they could be deceiving. Sure, Laverne was brash and opinionated, but she was also eager to help and fit in.

The next time Pastor Murphy asked her to meet with a potential resident, she vowed to go in with an open mind and give each one of them a fair shake. If the first meeting sent up red flags, Jo needed to give them a second chance and meet with them again before reaching a decision.

She could only imagine how stressful it was to be incarcerated. She thought about her mother. Jessica Carlton had never made it out of prison. She had died less than a decade after being convicted of murdering her husband, Jo's father.

The familiar and painful regrets from Jo's past swept over her. The long list of "what ifs" came flooding back. What if Jo had never returned home for that surprise visit? What if her father hadn't been home "entertaining" his latest girlfriend while her mother was out of town?

What if Jo had waited to confront her father and call her mother? What if she'd gone back to the house and been able to prevent the argument between her parents that had turned deadly?

Jo swallowed hard and briefly closed her eyes. She would give every penny of her inheritance to change the past. But it was too late. She had to keep reminding herself good *had* come from the bad.

The farm, and the women's lives that were being changed. And even now, a lonely farmer was getting a new lease on life.

She tweaked her message, sent it to the pastor and then wandered into the kitchen where she found Delta standing in front of the sink. "You're up and at 'em already."

"I couldn't sleep. I'm waiting for the deli to open. I remembered what it was about Sherry's attack that got my attention." Jo told her what it was.

"Seriously? I reckon that would make sense, but I don't get the why."

"Me either, which is what I'm hoping to find out." Jo waited until ten past seven to head to town. Thankfully, it was a Saturday morning, and since it was still early, there were only a handful of diners in the deli as Jo headed to the back, which is where she found her friend.

"Good morning, Jo. You're out early." Marlee grabbed a dishtowel and dried her hands. "How did your stakeout go?"

"It was basically a bust. Sherry remembered something about her attack. She heard a man call her name right before he struck her."

"A man," Marlee repeated. "So, it wasn't Nicole."

"No, which made me think of something else, something you said." Jo repeated what Marlee had told her, and her eyes grew round as saucers. "Oh, my gosh, Jo. You're right. I never even thought about that."

"Are you positive you didn't mention Sherry's attack to anyone, where the word might have gotten around right after it happened?"

"No." Marlee shook her head. "I'm positive. I didn't even tell the deli employees about it until later, when I knew she was going to be all right. What are you going to do?"

"Call Sheriff Franklin to meet me at the former mayor's home. I want a head start. I need to come up with an excuse for being there."

"I have an idea." Marlee dashed to the refrigerator. She removed a large pot of soup and placed it on the counter. "Troy Loughlin was in here last night, complaining he was feeling under the weather. You can deliver some homemade chicken noodle soup for me."

"How do you plan to get a confession?" Marlee filled a to-go container and placed a lid on top.

"I don't know. I'll think of something. How far away does he live?"

"Two blocks as the crow flies."

While Marlee placed crackers and napkins in a bag, Jo tracked down Loughlin's address and mapped it out using the walking app.

"Are you sure you want to do this alone?" Marlee handed Jo the container of soup and the brown bag.

"I'm not worried about him attacking me. By the time Loughlin realizes I'm onto him, the sheriff will be on the way."

"Be careful. If you don't come back within the hour, I'm going to come looking for you."

"It's a deal." Jo exited through the back, juggling the food in one hand and her cell phone in the other. Marlee's estimate about the distance was spot on, and Jo arrived at the tidy split-level home minutes later.

She studied the exterior, wondering if Loughlin was up or if she would be waking him. Either way, Jo's plan was to catch him off guard.

She climbed the front porch steps and reached for the doorbell when the landscaping around the front of the house caught her eye. She reached down and scooped up a small handful of white landscaping rocks.

Chapter 29

Jo tucked the small rocks in her front pocket and stepped off to the side. She dialed Sheriff Franklin's cell phone number. Her call went to voice mail. "Great," Jo muttered under her breath.

She left a brief message, asking him to call her back as soon as possible and then dialed the sheriff department's main number.

"Smith County Dispatch."

"Yes. This is Joanna Pepperdine. I'm looking for Sheriff Franklin. Is he on duty this morning?"

"He is."

Jo's phone beeped. It was Franklin. "Never mind. I have him on the other line." She disconnected and answered Franklin's call. "Thank you for getting back with me so quickly. I'm almost one hundred percent certain I know who has been harassing Sherry and who attacked her. It's Troy Loughlin."

There was a long pause on the other end of the line. "Former Mayor Loughlin? That's a strong accusation against an upstanding citizen of our community. Do you have proof?"

"Almost one hundred percent. I'm standing on Loughlin's front steps, getting ready to deliver some soup. You might want to get over here."

The sheriff told Jo he was on his way.

She timed it, waiting approximately three minutes before ringing the doorbell. The door slowly opened, and the man she'd seen inside the deli a couple days earlier appeared.

"Mr. Loughlin?"

"Yes."

Jo held up the container of food. "I have a special delivery from Marlee over at the deli. She said you were feeling under the weather, and I offered to drop this soup off on my way home."

"Thank you." He opened the door a crack and reached for the container.

"Sherry Marshall, one of the servers at the deli, is a former resident of mine." Jo saw a flicker of emotion. It quickly vanished.

"I know Sherry."

"She's waited on you before," Jo studied his face.

"She has."

"And you know she rented an apartment above Wayne Malton's hardware store."

"I believe I may have heard that."

Jo changed the subject. "I love your landscaping. I've been thinking about buying some of the same decorative white rocks for my flower gardens."

"They work well." The man shifted his gaze, looking over Jo's shoulder.

Jo turned, watching as the sheriff's patrol car pulled up alongside the curb.

Loughlin's eyes narrowed. "What's going on?"

Jo ignored the question as she removed one of the rocks from her pocket. "Someone has been harassing Sherry. In fact, she found a pile of these same white rocks on the roof, near her window ledge the other night."

"What does that have to do with me?"

Sheriff Franklin joined them. "Morning, Troy. You got me here, Ms. Pepperdine. Let's get down to business."

"I already am." Jo slowly turned to face Loughlin. "Someone attacked Sherry the other morning. It was a man. He called her name. When she turned, her attacker struck her in the head with a large wrench, which was found in the bushes nearby."

Loughlin's face turned ghostly pale. "I heard she was attacked."

"You *knew* she was attacked because you're the one who did it," Jo said.

"That...that's absurd," Loughlin blustered. "I don't know what you're talking about."

"Yes, you do. Do you want to know how I know?" Jo didn't wait for a reply. "Because you asked Marlee about Sherry's condition before the authorities were even notified. You were in the deli the morning of the attack, right after it opened and the incident occurred. The only people who knew about Sherry's attack other than me were Delta, Marlee, and Sherry's neighbor. How would you know about the attack unless you were the one who perpetrated it?"

Jo could feel her blood boil. "You've been stalking and harassing Sherry. It started with you just lurking around her place. It escalated when you started throwing rocks at her window. You damaged her mailbox, and finally, you attacked her."

"You're crazy," Loughlin grunted. "I heard rumors about you being a crazy woman, and now I believe it."

Sheriff Franklin joined Jo on the top step. "Mr. Loughlin is an upstanding citizen in our community, Ms. Pepperdine."

"I'm sure he is," Jo said. "Or was. I wouldn't be here if I wasn't certain he was behind the incidents."

The sheriff silently studied the look of determination on Jo's face before turning to the man standing in the doorway. "Since it's only a formality, and I'm sure Ms. Pepperdine will be happy to apologize if she's wrong, you wouldn't be opposed to running down to the station to provide us with a fingerprint sample to see if they match the one we found on the wrench, would you?"

"I will not. This is absurd." Loughlin straightened his shoulders. "My prints are not on the wrench."

Jo arched a brow. "Because you made sure you wiped it off before using it *and* you were wearing gloves. What would you say if Sheriff Franklin told you there was one small print found on the wrench?"

Loughlin's jaw dropped as the color drained from his face. He quickly recovered. "It's my word against hers."

"And Marlee Davison's," Jo said.

"I think this is a reasonable request, Troy." The sheriff placed a light hand on his radio.

"Not until I talk to my lawyer." Loughlin took a step back.

Certain that he was seconds away from slamming the door in their faces, Jo snatched the soup container from his hands and handed it to the sheriff. "I'm sure Mr. Loughlin's prints, which are on this container, will work just fine."

Loughlin lunged forward, attempting to grab the soup, but the sheriff was one step ahead of him and easily moved it out of his reach. "I think I'll hang onto this for now, Troy."

"I'll have your badge," Loughlin raged.

Jo could see the veins in his neck bulging out and wondered if he would attack her. Instead, he slammed the door in their faces.

"That was interesting. We're gonna have some egg on our faces if you're wrong, Ms. Pepperdine." The sheriff accompanied Jo to the end of the sidewalk and placed the soup container in a small bin on the floor of his patrol car. "I see you came on foot. Do you need a lift somewhere?"

"Sure. Can you drop me off at the deli? I promised Marlee I would let her know how this turned out."

"Even if your hunch is correct, it isn't over yet," the sheriff predicted. "Loughlin's got connections in this county. If you're right and he is responsible, I have a hunch he won't go down without a fight."

Chapter 30

"Well? What do you think?" Delta did a slow twirl, the hem of her dress rustling as she sashayed across the kitchen floor.

"It's beautiful." Jo ran a light hand over the silky blue material. "I don't believe I've ever seen you look so happy."

"Do you think Gary will like it?"

"Gary isn't going to like it. He's going to love it."

The front door banged shut, and Jo consulted the clock. "That must be the women. It won't be long until your guests start arriving." She shooed her friend out of the kitchen, passing by the residents who were making their way inside.

Laverne was notably absent from the group. "What happened to Laverne?"

"You mean Mad Scientist Laverne?" Raylene laughed. "She's in the kitchen, working on some super-secret surprise for Gary and Delta's engagement party. She wouldn't tell us what it was."

"Whatever it is, it smells good," Kelli said. "We're here to see if you're ready for us to start taking the food to the barn."

"I am." Jo and Nash had already assembled the tables and chairs early that morning. They had hung streamers and blown up balloons to give the barn a festive atmosphere. Jo brought in an Echo with Alexa and some speakers and managed to find time to create a special playlist of songs for the couple.

The women carried dish after dish of food and pitchers of beverages out the back door. There were salads and rolls, condiments, chips, dips, tea and lemonade. Nash had already placed the hamburger patties and hot dogs in a cooler, so they would be ready to go.

Gary, who brought his grill from home the day before, offered to help Nash with the grilling.

While the women assembled the food, Jo finished some last-minute prep work, slicing pickles and tomatoes, and chopping red onion for the hotdogs.

Sherry popped in as Jo was finishing up. "Sheriff Franklin and his wife are here."

"Good. Maybe he has some news about Troy Loughlin."

"He said he did, but he wanted to share it with both of us at the same time."

Jo hung her apron on the hook and followed Sherry out of the kitchen. The women worked their way through the crowd, stopping several times to greet guests.

They caught up with the sheriff and his wife outside the mercantile, chatting with Pastor Murphy.

"Hello, Ms. Pepperdine," the sheriff tipped his hat.

"I think we've reached the point where Jo might be more appropriate."

"Jo." The sheriff grasped the arm of the woman standing next to him. "This is my wife, Jeannie. Jeannie, this is Joanna Pepperdine."

The woman extended a hand. Her eyes were warm, and her smile friendly. "It's a pleasure to finally meet you. Bill said you're doing wonderful work here with the women."

"She is," Sherry said. "I'm one of the first to leave the farm and venture out on my own."

"Congratulations. If you have time, I'd love to have a tour of the facility."

"Absolutely, perhaps after things settle down," Jo turned to the sheriff. "Sherry said you had some news on her attack."

"You were right about Loughlin. His fingerprint matched the one we found on the wrench. He's claiming it's a setup. He's hired an attorney and is threatening to sue the department."

"That figures," Jo muttered. "Well, I still think he's responsible, whether he admits it or not. We may never know why he did it, although I have a hunch."

"Because he didn't want a former convict living in downtown Divine," Sherry said quietly.

"I'm sorry, Sherry," the sheriff apologized. "I personally believe he's guilty, but my hands are tied. You may be interested to know that Loughlin's putting his house up for sale. He's moving out of Divine."

"So, maybe the town is getting rid of the riff-raff after all," Pastor Murphy spoke.

"Yes, it appears you may be right. There's no place in Divine for people like that." Jo excused herself to track Nash down to begin grilling.

Delta nearly floated around as she showed off her engagement ring, her soon-to-be husband and shared the details of the upcoming wedding.

Jo and Nash waited until the food line cleared before filling their plates. They stood off to the side, surveying the crowd as they ate.

"Where's Laverne?" Nash asked. "I haven't seen her since the party began."

"Last I heard, she was in the women's kitchen working on a surprise." Jo polished off the rest of her hotdog. "I'll go see if I can track her down." She made her way to the common area and found Laverne standing at the kitchen counter, butter knife in hand. "There you are."

"Hi, Jo." Laverne shot Jo a quick glance. "This thing is taking longer than I planned."

"What is it?" Jo crossed the room and peered over Laverne's shoulder. She burst out laughing. "Oh, my gosh."

"Cool, huh? I have to say, even though it took longer than expected, it also turned out better than I thought it would."

"I think it's hilarious. I'm not sure how Delta will feel about it."

"You mean, she doesn't have a sense of humor?"

"It depends. It depends on what it is. She might like this, or she might not," Jo warned.

"I put a lot of work into my creation."

"Then we shall give it a go. Do you need some help?"

"Yes. If you can carry the cake knife and get the door." Laverne washed her hands in the sink before gingerly lifting the large sheet cake.

It was a slow go along the back, past the businesses and to the food table just inside the barn. Jo waited for Laverne to slide the cake onto the table and then placed the knife next to it. "Wait here. I'll track down Delta and Gary."

She found the couple chatting with Claire and Marlee and asked them to follow her for their first glimpse of Laverne's special surprise.

"Special surprise?" Delta eyed Jo suspiciously.

"She's been working on it since early this morning."

"I don't like that smirk on your face."

"It's all in good fun." Jo grasped her friend's hand and led her to the table. She snatched her cell phone from her pocket, getting ready for Delta's first glimpse of the custom, cream cheese frosting top.

"What?" Delta's jaw dropped.

Gary laughed. "I can see a clear resemblance."

"To me?" Delta shrieked.

"It's cute," Jo motioned for them to stand behind the cake. "I want to snap a picture before you cut into it."

Gary nearly dragged Delta behind the table. There was a deep scowl on her face, and no amount of cajoling could get her to crack a smile.

Jo snapped several pictures, making sure she got the entire scene, from the rolling pin in "Delta's" hand to Gary being dragged off his tractor to the rows of yellow sunflowers lining the gravel path leading off "into the sunset."

"Well?" Laverne clapped her hands. "What do you think?"

"I think it's adorable," Jo motioned to Laverne. "Get closer. We need a picture of the artist too."

Laverne's face lit up as she scooched closer to Delta.

"There. Got it," Jo said.

"That doesn't look like me," Delta grunted.

"I got a hankerin' for a piece of cake," Gary rubbed his hands. "It looks dee-licious."

The first dozen or so people were able to admire Laverne's creation, commenting on the creativity and joking about the look on Delta's face. Even she grudgingly admitted the lemon cream-filled cake with whipped cream cheese frosting was tasty.

Jo eased a generous slice of cake onto a small plate and brought it to Nash, who stood talking to their neighbor, Dave Kilwin. "This is for you."

There was a commotion near the barn doors, and Jo watched as a chicken began squawking loudly, wings flapping as it bolted across the driveway, desperately trying to escape. It left a trail of feathers behind as it took off across the yard.

Carrie Ford was hot on the bird's trail, chasing after it at an amazing speed, despite her leopard print stilettos. She finally caught the chicken and returned it to a nearby cage.

"What was that all about?" Nash shook his head.

Jo shrugged. "Who knows with Carrie."

Raylene ran over, her face bright red and looking like she was about to explode.

"What's up with the chicken?"

"Carrie Ford brought it with her. She remembered Leah saying she wanted to raise chickens, so she brought her one."

"Good grief." Jo slapped her forehead. "At least it's alive."

"I'm beginning to think the wedding is going to be the most exciting event of the year," Nash laughed.

"Year?" Jo briefly closed her eyes. "I'm thinking more along the lines of the decade."

The end.

If you enjoyed reading "Divine Courage," would you please take a moment to leave a review? It would mean so much. Thank you! - Hope

The series continues...Divine Cozy Mystery Series Book 7 Coming Soon!

Read More by Hope

Divine Cozy Mystery Series

After relocating to the tiny town of Divine, Kansas, strange and mysterious things begin to happen to businesswoman, Jo Pepperdine and those around her.

Garden Girls Cozy Mystery Series

A lonely widow finds new purpose for her life when she and her senior friends help solve a murder in their small Midwestern town.

Cruise Ship Cozy Mystery Series

A recently divorced senior lands her dream job as Assistant Cruise Director onboard a mega passenger cruise ship and soon discovers she's got a knack for solving murders.

Samantha Rite Mystery Series

Heartbroken after her recent divorce, a single mother is persuaded to book a cruise and soon finds herself caught in the middle of a deadly adventure. Will she make it out alive?

Made in Savannah Cozy Mystery Series

A mother and daughter try to escape their family's NY mob ties by making a fresh start in Savannah, GA but they soon realize you can run but you can't hide from the past.

Sweet Southern Sleuths Short Stories Series

Twin sisters with completely opposite personalities become amateur sleuths when a dead body is discovered in their recently inherited home in Misery, Mississippi.

Meet Hope Callaghan

Hope Callaghan is an American author who loves to write clean fiction books, especially Christian Mystery and Cozy Mystery books. She has written more than 70 mystery books (and counting) in six series.

In March 2017, Hope won a Mom's Choice Award for her book, "Key to Savannah," Book 1 in the Made in Savannah Cozy Mystery Series.

Born and raised in a small town in West Michigan, she now lives in Florida with her husband. She is the proud mother of 3 wonderful children.

When she's not doing the thing she loves best - writing books - she enjoys cooking, traveling and reading books.

Hope loves to connect with her readers! Connect with her today!

Never miss another book deal! From your mobile phone, Text the word: books to 33222

Click **hopecallaghan.com/newsletter** for special offers, books on sale, and soon-to-be-released books!

Follow Hope On These Social Channels:

Facebook:

https://www.facebook.com/authorhopecallaghan/

Amazon: https://www.amazon.com/Hope-Callaghan/e/B00OJ5X702/

Pinterest:

https://www.pinterest.com/cozymysteriesauthor/

Bonus Recipe

Delta's Peanut Butter Truffle Balls Recipe

Ingredients:

9 ounces (23) OREO Chocolate Sandwich Cookies, divided

4 oz. cream cheese, softened

8 oz. BAKER'S Semi-Sweet Baking Chocolate, melted

½ cup peanut butter

Directions:

-Crush five of the cookies to fine crumbs in food processor; reserve for later use. (Cookies can also be finely crushed in a resealable plastic bag using a rolling pin.)

-Crush the remaining 18 cookies. Place in medium bowl.

-Add softened cream cheese and peanut butter; mix

until well blended.

-Roll cookie mixture into 24 balls, about 1-inch in diameter.

-Freeze or chill batter. (about 25 minutes)

-Dip balls in melted chocolate; place on wax paper-covered baking sheet. (Using two forks. Let excess chocolate drip off.)

-Sprinkle with reserved cookie crumbs.

-Refrigerate until firm, about 1 hour.

-Store leftover truffles, covered, in refrigerator.

*Makes approx. 24 truffles

Made in the USA
Thornton, CO
07/15/23 13:08:58

75bf1159-7d5a-4afb-a157-a8b2162776c1R01